LOVE UNDER FIRE

Barbara Cartland

Barbara Cartland Ebooks Ltd

This edition © 2018

ISBNs

9781788670593   EPUB

9781788670609   PAPERBACK

Book design by M-Y Books
m-ybooks.co.uk

THE BARBARA CARTLAND ETERNAL COLLECTION

The Barbara Cartland Eternal Collection is the unique opportunity to collect all five hundred of the timeless beautiful romantic novels written by the world's most celebrated and enduring romantic author.

Named the Eternal Collection because Barbara's inspiring stories of pure love, just the same as love itself, the books will be published on the internet at the rate of four titles per month until all five hundred are available.

The Eternal Collection, classic pure romance available worldwide for all time .

THE LATE DAME BARBARA CARTLAND

Barbara Cartland, who sadly died in May 2000 at the grand age of ninety eight, remains one of the world's most famous romantic novelists. With worldwide sales of over one billion, her outstanding 723 books have been translated into thirty six different languages, to be enjoyed by readers of romance globally.

Writing her first book 'Jigsaw' at the age of 21, Barbara became an immediate bestseller. Building upon this initial success, she wrote continuously throughout her life, producing bestsellers for an astonishing 76 years. In addition to Barbara Cartland's legion of fans in the UK and across Europe, her books have always been immensely popular in the USA. In 1976 she achieved the unprecedented feat of having books at numbers 1 & 2 in the prestigious B. Dalton Bookseller bestsellers list.

Although she is often referred to as the 'Queen of Romance', Barbara Cartland also wrote several historical biographies, six autobiographies and numerous theatrical plays as well as books on life, love, health and cookery. Becoming one of Britain's most popular media personalities and dressed in her trademark pink, Barbara spoke on radio and television about social and political issues, as well as making many public appearances.

In 1991 she became a Dame of the Order of the British Empire for her contribution to literature and her work for humanitarian and charitable causes.

Known for her glamour, style, and vitality Barbara Cartland became a legend in her own lifetime. Best remembered for her wonderful romantic novels and loved by millions of readers worldwide, her books remain treasured for their heroic heroes, plucky heroines and traditional values. But above all, it was Barbara Cartland's overriding belief in the positive power of love to help, heal and improve the quality of life for everyone that made her truly unique.

AUTHOR'S NOTE

I would like my readers to know that the details of life with Napoleon's Armies are as accurate as research can make them. The fog that descended on the Maya Pass in July was an actual phenomenon in 1813.

CHAPTER ONE
1813

"No! *No*! – Please don't hit me again – spare me! – spare me!"

The girl's voice ended in a shriek of pain as the whip descended with an even greater force and she collapsed on the floor sobbing bitterly.

One last lash and then the woman holding the whip flung it with all her strength against the wall.

"That will teach you, you little fool," she stormed, "to let your father get into such a state."

"It w-was not m-my fault," the girl sobbed. "He sent me – away when his friends called – to s-see him."

"Excuses! Always excuses," the woman standing over her muttered. "What am I to do now? How can I go to the ball without him?"

Seeing that the tempest had abated a little, the girl lying on the floor raised herself cautiously. Tears were streaming down her small pointed face. The hazel eyes she regarded her persecutor with held no enmity and no bitterness.

She was used to such beatings for her stepmother's temper was proverbially turbulent and when things went wrong she always had to take it out on someone.

Elvina was the nearest and easiest person to wreak her anger on and invariably the girl received the full brunt of it

'What can I do? *What can I do*?' Mistress Lake asked.

She moved across the room to the window to stand looking out with a frown between her dark eyes while she drummed her long thin fingers on the windowsill.

The daughter of a Portuguese father and a French mother, Juanita, the second wife of Major George Lake, late of the fifth Regiment, had been a beauty when she first married.

But the privations of war, her husband's ill health since his leg had been amputated and his incessant bouts of drinking had left her lined and querulous with a disgruntled down-turned mouth and frantic bursts of ill-temper that at times seemed to bring her almost to the verge of madness.

Elvina was terrified of her stepmother.

At the same time she had learned with a certain philosophical common sense to accept the beatings that she received all too frequently as something that must be endured for no other reason than that she could not escape them.

Very small and thin owing to the lack of nourishment over these past formative and growing years, she looked little more than a child who should be in the nursery when, in reality, she had just passed her seventeenth birthday.

Now, as she gathered herself up from the floor and smoothed down the skirts of her faded and worn gown, she gave a little murmur of pain from the soreness of her back and shoulders and saw that a weal on her arm was bleeding where the whip had broken the skin.

"What am I to do?" Mistress Lake asked from the window.

"I cannot think," Elvina answered, "unless you go without him."

The frown between her stepmother's eyes lightened for a moment.

"Dare I? What would people think? What would they say?"

"I hardly think they would notice," Elvina pointed out.

"I could say he was ill," Mistress Lake said. "That is true enough. Or I could tell the truth," she added bitterly, "and say that he is lying in a drunken sodden stupor from which nothing, not even the arrival of the French, would awaken him."

"I wish I could come with you," Elvina said a little wistfully.

Her stepmother laughed unpleasantly.

"That would indeed be to invite comment. A nice scarecrow you would look in your old clothes. Besides you have not been invited and I have told you often enough that you never will be asked to any of these parties so long as I can prevent it. I did not bargain, when I married your father, for having to chaperone a girl almost as old as I am myself."

This was a palpable lie and they both knew it. Juanita Lake was over thirty, but she always spoke of herself as if she was a mere girl.

Tactfully ignored was the fact that she had only married an Englishman because no one in Lisbon wished to espouse a girl who had not only no dowry but a French mother to boot.

She slammed her hand down with a sudden crash on the windowsill.

"I shall go alone," she declared. "It is decided! I shall throw myself on the mercy of the first good-looking man I see and ask him to be my escort into the ballroom. Who knows? Lord Wye himself might see fit to befriend me."

"It will be a wonderful ball," Elvina said wistfully, rubbing her arms, which had begun to ache intolerably.

"The finest ball ever seen in Lisbon," Juanita Lake answered. "And why not? When a messenger arrived with the news that the Duke of Wellington had defeated the French at Vitoria and gained a famous victory, I declare my heart almost stopped beating for joy."

Juanita always exaggerated her patriotism for fear that people should remember her French blood.

Half her ill-temper came from her embarrassment in bearing enemy blood and her fears that people would constantly be talking about her.

She made few friends and when, by any chance, her overtures to new acquaintances were disregarded or misunderstood, she beat Elvina to relieve her feelings.

Then, as often as not, she wept wild, bitter hysterical tears, declaring that she hated everybody and everything in this accursed war-ridden country.

Food had been very short for years, but now, with the British continually landing new consignments of troops in Lisbon and with the hope and excitement engendered by the Duke of Wellington's recent victories, things were better.

The peasants no longer hoarded everything for themselves. There were vegetables, fruit and game for sale in the market and fresh bread was baked every day.

Elvina could remember when it was not a question of having no money, but of being unable to buy anything with it.

Now money was the only difficulty. Unfortunately, as far as the household was concerned, Juanita took everything that was available, for Major Lake was too drunk or too indolent to care what happened to his pension.

As long as he had enough to drink that was all that mattered to him and, as his credit was good and he had innumerable friends in the town, he at least was content to drink and forget his domestic troubles.

It was becoming obvious to Elvina that he forgot her too.

"What is going to happen to me, Papa?" she had asked him only a week earlier.

He had been more sober than usual, but he stared at her, puckering his brow as if he was not only trying to understand what she was saying but also to remember who she was.

"I cannot stay like this for ever," she went on. "I am growing up and yet I am never allowed to go out to meet anyone. I have no friends. I am only a servant to Juanita, as you well know."

For a moment Major George Lake had the grace to look ashamed.

"Things have been difficult owing to the War," he muttered. "Your stepmother gets overwrought."

"Yes, I know," Elvina said patiently. "But the news is better. People talk of the War being over before the end of the year."

"With Napoleon still the conqueror of Europe?" Major Lake asked derisively. "There is not a chance."

"Well, perhaps next year then," Elvina persisted. "But I am seventeen, Father, and I feel that I should be thinking of other things besides housework and mending Juanita's clothes. She will not even allow me to have a new gown for myself."

"I will speak to her," Major Lake replied hastily.

But he averted his eyes as he spoke so that his daughter knew that he would do nothing of the sort.

He was afraid of his second wife and indeed they both were.

"I do *not* think it is for Juanita to decide my future," Elvina went on. "That is for you, Papa. When the War is over, would it be possible for me to go back to England? Surely some of my mother's relations must still be alive."

"If they are, they have made no effort to get in touch with me," Major Lake said angrily. "I was not good enough for their daughter. Oh, no! They wanted somebody better for her. 'Who is this fellow, Lake?' they asked, looking down their long noses. Well I would rot in Hell before I would ask them for a penny piece."

He was not as sober as Elvina had thought.

As he grew angry, his voice thickened and now lurching towards the door, he passed through it, slamming it behind him.

Elvina sank down on a chair and covered her face with her hands. What was to be the end of it all? Sometimes, remembering her mother, she felt that she could go on no longer.

Then the house had been clean and pretty, filled with flowers, sunshine and happiness.

They had moved here five years ago in 1808 from Gibraltar where her father had been stationed ever since he married. Elvina could remember their home there, but her most vivid memories were of Lisbon.

She could see her mother now, coming through the door, her fair hair like a halo around her pretty face and Elvina would run to meet her.

"Elvina, my darling!" she would say and clasp her close to her heart.

Elvina felt the tears drop from her eyes onto her fingers.

Why, she asked in her heart, could she not have died as well of the cholera that, brought by the wounded and dying back from the front line where the French were driving their enemies irresistibly before them, had swept the City.

She could remember her father going off with his Regiment, looking tall and handsome and in the best of spirits.

"Don't cry, my pretty," he had said to her mother. "We will beat Boney and I will be back with you before you realise I have gone."

But he had returned to a house empty of his wife and to lie himself between life and death for several months.

"The French are invincible! We will never beat them. It's hopeless to try," he would say despondently.

This depressed the new recruits as they came out from England and cast such a gloom over the dinner parties that many of his old cronies ceased to entertain him.

It was then, to regain his spirits and relieve his pain, that he took to drink. And during one of his more drunken bouts he brought home his new wife.

If Elvina had been quite unprepared to be presented with a stepmother, it had been no consolation to find that Juanita was just as unpleasantly surprised.

"You told me you had a child, but I thought it was only a few years old," she said to her husband.

She looked distastefully at Elvina, aged fourteen, who stood awkwardly staring at the dark-eyed and over-dressed woman her father had just announced to her as a new mother.

"Come, you must be friends," Major Lake said jovially.

He had reached the stage in his drinking when the entire world seemed glorious and everyone was his friend.

"Kiss each other. You will enjoy each other's company," he urged, while Elvina, looking fearfully into the new Mistress Lake's eyes, saw that there only scorn and hatred.

Yet however much she might dislike another female in the house and however much she might beat and persecute her wretched stepdaughter, there were times when Juanita must talk to Elvina because there was no one else.

This was one of them.

"I will go alone!" she said. "But, supposing, just supposing, no one speaks to me."

"But they will," Elvina insisted.

She knew all too well these moments of depression and false humility when her stepmother believed that the whole world was against her.

"You know so many people," she went on. "Besides, everyone will be in good spirits. There is so much to celebrate."

Juanita smiled and for a moment the darkness fled from her eyes.

"There is, indeed," she said. "I hear today that after the battle on the road to Pamplona they captured the treasure wagons and carriages that King Joseph was fleeing from Madrid in."

"The treasure wagons!" Elvina exclaimed. "Was there much in them?"

"There was money, jewellery, pictures and furniture and fine clothes!" Juanita answered. "The Army feasted on food and wine that King Joseph and the women of the Court had provided themselves with for their journey. How I wish I could have been there. I should not have come away empty handed."

"I hear a lot of men were slain in the battle," Elvina commented quietly.

"You cannot have War without casualties," Juanita answered. "Don't let us bother our heads with it. Are you quite certain that my gown is ready for tonight?"

"It is ready," Elvina replied.

No one knew better than she did that that was the truth. She had been up half the night altering it, pressing the lace, mending the satin underskirt and sewing on new ribbons.

No woman in Lisbon had had a new gown for years.

They did the best they could with their old gowns, altering them according to the out of date reports which sometimes seeped through of the fashions in Paris or begging newly arrived Officers from England to tell them what was the vogue in St. James's and what the Prince Regent's many *amorettas* wore at Carlton House.

The ball tonight was to be given in the Palace on the waterfront and all day long the City had been in a state of excitement at the thought of such unusual festivity.

"Who is Lord Wye?" Elvina asked as she brought Juanita's gown from a cupboard and laid it on the bed.

"A rich English Milord," Juanita answered with a shrug of her shoulders. "The type of man I should have married had I not let myself be persuaded into the madness of giving my hand to your father."

Elvina had nothing to say to this.

She knew only too well that her father had been Juanita's last hope of matrimony and that she had married him at a moment's notice before he had had time to sober up and think better of his proposal.

In fact privately Elvina was always convinced that her father's proposal to Juanita, if indeed he had made one, had never meant a permanent alliance, but one that he had suggested to so many ladies and which, in his own words, 'was strictly dishonourable'.

"Now fetch my mantilla, my comb and my fan. Get everything ready," Juanita demanded imperiously.

Meekly Elvina went to obey her. She always acted as lady's maid to Juanita and was used to being ordered about without any question of thanks.

As she crossed the room, there was a sudden noise of cheering from outside and involuntarily both women ran to the window.

The small paned window with its ornate iron grille overlooked the narrow street with a dirty gutter running down the middle. There were always a number of starving diseased beggars sitting on the doorsteps or slouching against the walls.

These were being reinforced at the moment by a lot of people running and crowding out of the houses and coming from other streets to see who was approaching.

"It must be the new visitors," Juanita cried, bending forward.

Two horses, with a shine on their coats and in perfect condition, were being ridden down the road.

Behind them came a closed carriage followed by a detachment of soldiers obviously new arrivals from England with their red coats, bright accoutrements and white breeches.

Riding the leading horses were two gentlemen dressed in the height of fashion, one an elderly man, the other young and good-looking with a bronzed face which seemed to set off the blue of his coat and the snowy whiteness of his cravat.

"Who are they?" Elvina breathed.

"Our guests for tonight," Juanita answered, her eyes glittering. "The elder is the Ambassador, the new Ambassador, I had heard that he was expected. And the other must be Lord Wye."

He was certainly distinguished, Elvina thought, broad-shouldered and handsome enough to justify the sudden expression of yearning in Juanita's face and, indeed in the faces of the other women crowding in the windows opposite and in the street below.

They were not used to such good looks or such a dandified appearance in Lisbon.

There was little pageantry now about Wellington's Army. The men, if they were not wounded, were bronzed, tough and wiry from constant marching and even more constant fighting, but never had an Army looked less smart.

The powder, the clay pipe, the shining brass work and brilliant clothes of peacetime England had vanished.

Their jackets were faded and ragged, their breeches patched with old blankets and their shakos twisted into strange shapes and bleached by the sun.

Their Commander-in-Chief did not worry, so long as they kept their weapons in good order and brought sixty rounds of ammunition into the field.

A man might look like a scarecrow, but if he had kept his firelock bright and clean, he was a good soldier.

These gentlemen from England looked so different. Their polished boots, their snowy breeches and cravats, their gloved hands and even the way that they sat on their horses, all seemed different. No wonder the crowds were cheering.

"If only I had a new gown," Juanita said. "Once men thought I was beautiful. But what chance do I have in this old rag?"

Elvina did not answer. She hardly heard her. She was looking at Lord Wye and thinking that here was an Englishman such as her father must once have been. A gentleman proud and independent and sure of himself.

Very different from the raw recruits who came tumbling off the ships, often green and shaken after a bad passage in the Bay of Biscay, or the old veterans who greeted them and who seemed at times almost indistinguishable from their slouching dark-skinned Portuguese allies.

That was how an Englishman should look, Elvina told herself. Sure of himself and yet kindly to those around him.

There had been nothing disdainful in Lord Wye's glance at the people thronging the streets and there was nothing condescending in his smile. And yet he had seemed as much apart from them as if he had arrived from another planet or from Mount Olympus itself.

What would he be like to talk to, Elvina wondered.

What would he say? Would his conversation be very different from that of any other man?

Her father's cronies, the Portuguese Officials who came sometimes to the house or the members of the aristocracy whom she saw driving through the town, seeming by their very expressions to ignore the poverty and the dirt and the squalor that existed around them.

On an impulse Elvina turned towards her stepmother.

"Let me come with you tonight," she said. "I will not be a nuisance, I promise you. And you could explain that as my father is ill I have taken his place. I could make myself a gown in the time. There is that old blue of yours that you no longer care for. I could cover it with a layer of gauze and sew on a few new ribbons. Please – let me."

Juanita Lake stared at her in amazement.

"Have you taken leave of your senses?" she asked at length. "Do you think I want to arrive with another woman? I, who have always been escorted by men. Besides, as I have told you before, for me you don't exist except as my servant, someone who obeys my orders. There is no place in my household for other people's children. It is I who am important, I who am supreme in my own house. So get that into your head."

She walked across to Elvina and, taking her by the shoulders turned, her round to face the light from the window.

"So it is Englishmen you are after, is it?" she said stormingly. "Let me tell you this. When you get a little older, I am turning you out! I am not a fool that I can see that with your fair hair and your English complexion you are going to show up the wrinkles that are coming to my face. In another year out you will go and no amount of pleading or crying will save you."

She gave an unpleasant laugh.

"I shall not care what becomes of you. The camp up the road will welcome you doubtless or you can go and die on the nearest dunghill. So remember that when you start asking me to let you go to the ball."

She slapped Elvina's face with the palm of her hand and then, turning towards the dressing table, unbound her long dark hair and started to comb it.

For a moment Elvina stood staring at her, the tears starting to her eyes from the force of the blow. Slowly she put up her hands toward her burning cheek.

"Hot water, clean towels, my stockings and petticoats!" Juanita commanded.

Automatically Elvina sprang to obey the harsh order, and even as she scurried about the house, fetching first this and then that for her stepmother, her mind was all the time concerned with the threats that she had just listened to.

Juanita meant them. Elvina was not such a fool as not to know the truth when she heard it. She knew now that this was what Juanita had always intended, to be rid of her some way or another.

She wondered wildly what she could do.

To appeal to her father was hopeless.

She had only to go downstairs to see him lying on the sofa, dead drunk, an overturned wine glass on the floor beside him, to know that anything she told him would be forgotten the next time he opened a bottle.

What was she to do?

The question seemed to run through her head all the time she was helping Juanita wash and make up her face and she fastened her into her gown, arranging her hair in what they both imagined was the latest fashion and clasping round her neck the few tawdry bits of jewellery that had not been sold to pay bills or obtain wine.

"Your father was saying something the other night about a locket with diamonds in it," Juanita said unexpectedly.

Elvina was suddenly very still.

"Do you know what he was talking about?" Juanita enquired.

"N-no, I have – no idea."

"I suspect it was a locket that belonged to your mother. Were there diamonds round it?"

"I-I don't – know. I – don't – remember it."

"If you are lying to me, I will beat you until your bones stick out of your body," Juanita grunted.

"I will – have a search for it, if you like, and see – if I can find it," Elvina suggested.

"You can do it tonight. Search everywhere, your father's room and the trunks that were your mother's. There is not much left in them, but it may still be there. It will keep you busy while I am away."

Juanita rose to her feet. She stared at her reflection in the mirror and gave a little laugh of satisfaction.

"I have the feeling that I shall enjoy myself at the ball," she said. "I am still good-looking. I still have the power to attract men, I am sure of it. That is all that is really necessary to be sure of oneself and of one's own beauty."

She turned round, looked at herself from another angle and smiled again.

"Is the carriage here?"

"I told you twenty minutes ago that it had arrived."

"You may have the privilege of coming downstairs and handing me into it," Juanita said. "As I have no gentleman to escort me, I must make the best use of what I have. If your father wakes, tell him he will learn what I think of his behaviour tomorrow."

She turned towards the door.

"And as for you," she said, her voice ominous, "If that locket is not found, you will know what to expect!"

Elvina watched the carriage drive away and then let the old man, who had served her father ever since he came to Lisbon and who was partially deaf, close the front door.

She went upstairs to her own room. It was a small attic at the very top of the house, it was hot in summer and cold in winter and was therefore not considered good enough for any of the servants.

She shut herself in and, kneeling down in one corner of the room, pulled up a loose floorboard and took a small bundle from under it.

In it were all her treasures, a lock of her mother's hair, a locket and a bow of ribbon that had fallen from one of her gowns and which Elvina had secreted away before

Juanita had noticed its loss, a tiny gold ring that her mother had worn on her little finger, and the locket.

It was wrapped in paper, which Elvina undid with trembling fingers.

It was not large and the diamonds that surrounded it were not of great intrinsic value. But the locket itself was the most precious thing in the whole of Elvina's life, for it contained, the only likeness she possessed of her mother.

Beautifully painted on ivory, the round young face with its blue eyes and fair hair, seemed almost that of an angel.

For a long time Elvina stared at it.

Then she kissed it gently and lifting the chain hung it round her neck. She was so small, or else the locket had been intended for a much larger person, that it hung low between her breasts and was hidden from sight.

She slipped the ring onto her little finger and put back the floorboard so that anyone entering the room would not notice that it had been moved.

Often at night she wore the things that had been her mother's, but she had believed until this evening that her father had forgotten their existence and certainly she had not spoken to him of the locket for many years.

Now she was afraid. Juanita had a way of getting what she wanted, either by brutality or else by almost hypnotising things out of those who were afraid of her.

With her back sore from her beating, with her arms hurting her and the tears still wet in her eyes, Elvina felt a kind of peace come over her from the very moment that her mother's possessions touched her skin.

She went to the window. It was only small and the street seemed a long way below. Yet the stars were nearer, coming out into the darkening sky as night began to fall.

It was then that a sudden idea came to her and jumping up she took a shawl from where it was hanging on a nail behind the door and, pulling it over her head, she went downstairs.

The house was in darkness for there was no point in wasting the precious and expensive candles on a man who was too drunk to see them and a girl who should have gone to bed supperless. Elvina felt her way along the familiar passages until she reached the door that led to the kitchen.

Old José might be sitting there and might ask her where she was going, but she had the idea that he would be out in the streets, drinking with his compatriots or staring at the guests proceeding to the ball at the Palace.

For fear she might be heard, however, she went on tiptoe until she saw that the kitchen too was in darkness and then, growing bolder, she pulled open the back door and let herself out into the street.

Here there was confusion and excitement.

The narrow streets were filled with people of all descriptions, gaping Redcoats who must just have arrived from England, Portuguese carrying guitars to twang beneath the windows where dark-eyed ladies, half-hidden in the shadows, would be waiting for them.

There were crowds of small beggar boys in rags and with bare feet holding out thin, bony little hands to anyone they encountered and begging monotonously for bread or alms.

There were peasants who had come in from the countryside because they had heard of the battle and who stared about them curiously afraid, as they had been for over ten years, of what would happen to them next.

But above the smell of the crowds, the dust and the slop-pails that were continually being emptied into the gutters, there was the scent of aloe and cypress, of orange groves and of rosemary and thyme growing in the gardens of the houses or being carried on the wind from the wild land beyond the confines of the town.

Elvina hurried along in the shadows. She was so small that no one noticed her and indeed she was used to moving unobtrusively about the town.

She soon found her way to the seafront and to the great white Palace surrounded by its gardens. Through the ornamental gates the carriages were passing in a long line.

Outside there were crowds of beggars and peasants pressing forward eagerly to catch a glimpse of the guests. It was a rare chance to see gentlemen wearing their decorations and orders beside women half-naked in their finery, their dark eyes flashing with excitement, their lips as red as the roses that many of them had arranged in their hair.

Elvina, however, avoided the gates and moved away towards the back of the Palace. This was old familiar ground for she often came here to be alone.

There was a spot where the top of the wall had crumbled and she could climb over into the Palace gardens.

Often she would sneak in and sit here alone and undisturbed when Juanita thought that she was shopping or when she knew that to return to the house would be to receive yet another beating for something which she had done or left undone.

The great rambling Palace gardens, neglected because all the young gardeners who tended them had gone to the War, were the one place where Elvina could feel at peace and know that she would not be disturbed.

Tonight she was not too sure that she could enter unperceived. But the sentries were not expecting strangers and were far too engaged with watching what was going on themselves to suspect that anyone might enter the grounds except by the main entrance.

With the help of an almond tree which she had used so often before, Elvina hoisted herself on top of the wall at the place where the sharp spikes, intended to repulse thieves, had long since fallen down, and let herself down on to the other side.

Here there was soft grass beneath her feet, the fragrance of roses and flowering shrubs that brushed against her swollen and bruised shoulders and seemed to heal her by the very delicacy and gentleness of their touch.

She moved slowly through the gardens, keeping in the shrubbery and behind the yew hedges until she came within sight of The Palace.

Then she stopped. Every window was a blaze of light. She could see the glittering chandeliers filled with candles and guests moving under them to the strains of an orchestra.

The music was sweet and melodious and, fascinated, Elvina drew a little nearer. Never had she imagined that people could look so beautiful in the candlelight.

There was jewellery glistening round the necks and on the heads of the women and the men seemed equally resplendent in their coloured coats, high white cravats and diamond-studded orders.

The music seemed almost hypnotic, as did the figures moving in time to it. Then, suddenly Elvina became aware that two people were walking from The Palace into the gardens, picking their way between the rose beds almost to where she was standing.

Hastily she ducked behind a shrub and crept along close to the ground until she was sheltered by a little arbour covered with climbing roses where there was a seat arranged with satin cushions.

"Shall we sit down?" she heard a man's voice say.

"That would be lovely," a woman replied. "It's so hot inside. I am sure your Lordship must find it stifling after the cold of England."

"You will recall that it was not so very cold when we left," the man answered. "Although I admit the climate is much warmer here."

"Don't play with me, we have so little time," the woman said quickly. "Must you return tomorrow?"

The question was almost whispered.

"I am afraid so," the man replied. "As you know I only came to bring dispatches for the Duke of Wellington and certain letters for members of the Government."

The woman sighed.

"We were unable to talk when the sea was so rough, can you not stay just a little longer?"

"I wish I could, but there is work for me to do in England."

"We well know that the chief work that your Lordship is engaged on is to try and make the Prince Regent a little more popular with the people and more amenable to his Ministers!"

The man threw back his head and laughed.

"Your Ladyship must have been listening to the most flattering and ill-informed gossip."

"On the contrary, my sources of information are impeccable," the woman said. "Please, I beg you, stay a little longer."

Elvina knew, without being able to see the couple who were speaking, that the woman laid her hand on the man's arm.

Very very cautiously she raised her head.

They were sitting with their backs to her and she saw the man take the woman's hand and raise her fingers to his lips.

"If I could stay, I would," he answered.

The woman gave a sound that was almost one of exasperation and took her hand away.

"So, like many others, I have been refused by the all-conquering but elusive Lord Wye."

He laughed again.

"You know me well enough to be sure that is not true. I would like to stay. I would like, above all things, to join Wellington's army. But the Prime Minister's instructions were explicit. I was to return immediately."

"We had hoped to tempt you to defy the Prime Minister."

"I know, your husband said the same thing. It was indeed gracious of you both. But my yacht has been replenished with provisions and water and unless the wind fails me, we sail at dawn."

"So, we shall not meet again?"

"We shall meet in England."

"And how long have we to wait for that? Oh, my dear man, have you any idea how many bruised and unhappy hearts you leave behind you everywhere you go?"

"Again you are flattering me," Lord Wye said.

"I wish I was," she said, a little sob in her voice. "But I have to remain in this horrible, dirty, flea-ridden country while you return to civilisation."

"You must not be too hard on our oldest ally," Lord Wye said gently. "The Portuguese have suffered greatly from the last six years of War. Did you see those children at the dock today? They were little skeletons. I wish I could feed them."

"I am not interested in Portuguese children!" the woman exclaimed petulantly, "but in *you*!"

"I am deeply honoured by your interest in me."

"If I could only believe that," she sighed. "But we must go back. We might be missed and besides there are a great many Portuguese dignitaries you have not yet spoken to. You must not leave behind a bad impression."

"No indeed I am trying to leave a good one," he asserted.

She gave another sob and now her face was raised to his. For a moment he looked down at her.

To Elvina they were both in silhouette against the light streaming from The Palace.

Then Lord Wye bent and kissed his companion lightly. Just for a moment his lips touched hers and then, as she would have clung to him, he rose to his feet.

"We must go back," he said.

Elvina could almost feel the despair that, like an arrow, seemed to pass through the woman at his side.

Then a sudden pride made her lift her chin high.

"I hope I may give you one more dance before you go," she said.

"I shall insist on it," Lord Wye replied.

They walked back to The Palace the way they had come and Elvina gazed after them until they passed out of sight.

Then she rose to her feet and quite suddenly she knew what she must do.

She slipped back over the wall the way she had come, slithered down the almond tree and ran as quickly as her legs could carry her back home.

A drunken soldier snatched at her as she flashed by, but she eluded him. Some small boys called after her, but she hardly heard them.

As she reached the house, she intended to awaken old José, but he was not back and the door was still ajar as she had left it. She went into the kitchen and, after kindling a light from a taper, found in the cupboard what she was looking for.

It was a bottle of walnut juice that Juanita had made her prepare a few weeks earlier for staining the boards where the sun had faded them.

She hurried upstairs, seeking in Juanita's room for another bottle. It was full of dark liquid that her stepmother kept her hair raven black with.

Elvina took both bottles to her own attic bedchamber.

Here she pulled her shawl from her head and in the cracked mirror that stood on her chest of drawers she stared at herself for a moment.

Her fair hair, the same colour as her mother's, waved softly until it reached to her waist.

Taking a pair of scissors, she began to cut it off!

CHAPTER TWO

Lord Wye, looking surprisingly fresh considering that he had gone to bed at six o'clock in the morning and had less than an hour's sleep, gave the order to cast off.

The Officials and members of the Ambassador's household, who had also risen to bid him 'farewell', stood in a little group on the quay and saluted as the sailors dragged up the anchor and started to unfurl and set the sails.

Lord Wye noted that one of the *aides-de-camp* was yawning and another was still unsteady on his feet.

He wondered why they had all stayed so late at what in reality had been a very indifferent ball and then chided himself for being uncharitable.

A ball was an event in this war-stricken land and he, satiated with the glories of Carlton House and the Season in London, had no right to criticise.

He looked wistfully towards the hills overshadowing the town and wished that he had been able to defy the Prime Minister's orders and join Wellington's army, as he had begged to be allowed to do.

"No, Wye!" the Prime Minister had said firmly. "I wish you to deliver the letters that I entrust to your care to the Government of Portugal. Since Prince John sailed for Rio de Janeiro six years ago the Regency has changed hands continually and yet somehow the country keeps going and the Portuguese people have been stalwart and strong in the face of the French assaults. Wellington speaks highly of their soldiers, although he cannot trust them to take the initiative, but only to support our own troops."

"Do you not think," Lord Wye had suggested, "that it might be a good idea for me to have a word with the Duke of Wellington? He might wish to entrust me with communications for you that it would be difficult for him to put in his dispatches."

"Wellington's dispatches will be waiting for you at Lisbon," the Prime Minister said firmly. "I wish you to come straight back. The Prince Regent will miss you sorely and you know how difficult he can be if he has not the right advisers at his side."

The Prime Minister sighed and there was no need to say more. The Prince Regent was a continual problem.

Yet when, as occasionally happened, he took a fancy to someone who was acceptable to his Ministers, then a sigh of relief went up in Westminster that was echoed all over the Capital.

The question as to how long Lord Wye would last was the only damper on the general jubilation.

As far as the Prime Minister was concerned, he was not going to risk Lord Wye's most Diplomatic handling of the Prince Regent by letting him remain abroad a moment longer than was necessary.

"If there was anyone else I could send, I would not employ your Lordship on this mission," he said. "As it is, you are to proceed to Lisbon and come back here again with all possible speed. Do you think you are wise to use your own yacht? I would prefer to put a Warship at your disposal."

"If you want speed, my yacht will outpace a Warship by a dozen knots," Lord Wye replied, "besides being easier to take in and out of Harbour. What is more, the Admiralty are being hard pressed to provide enough troop ships. I think you would make me very unpopular, sir, if you insisted on providing a Warship for my use at this particular moment."

"Very well then, go in your own yacht," the Prime Minister conceded. "I understand you are taking Sir Horace Bowhill and his lady with you."

"They have done me the honour to be my guests on the voyage," Lord Wye replied.

"And being a very pretty woman Lady Bowhill will undoubtedly relieve the monotony of the days at sea, eh?"

The Prime Minister's eyes twinkled.

An unattractive man himself, he always had a sneaking respect for good-looking buccaneers like Lord Wye, who swept every woman they met off their feet and about them there was always some spicy piece of scandal being tittered at in the Clubs and salons.

Had the Prime Minister but known it, Lady Bowhill had proved a disappointment.

Now, as his yacht began to move out into the open sea, Lord Wye thought with relief that on the homeward voyage he would be alone.

'Women,' he said to himself, 'are all right so long as you can get away from them. They can be a damned nuisance in a confined space.'

He contemplated with satisfaction the emptiness of the cabin and settling himself on a comfortable high-backed chair, began to read with interest some of the papers that had been given him at Lisbon for conveyance to England.

They included an angry demand for more cavalry horses and a complaint that the last consignment of sugar had been mixed with sand.

Engrossed in what he was reading Lord Wye did not hear a knock on the door and looked up to find that the Captain of the yacht had entered the cabin and was standing opposite him waiting for his attention.

"Anything I can do for you, Captain?" Lord Wye enquired.

"I only came to warn you, my Lord, that the weather looks unpleasant. It's likely to be very rough outside the Harbour, the wind appears to be getting up and the sky promises a storm."

"Well, it was pretty rough in the Bay coming out," Lord Wye replied. "I don't know what has happened to the weather this year. One does not expect tempests at the beginning of July."

"I agree with you, my Lord," the Captain replied. "But remember the equinoctial gales last year. They strewed the Channel with wrecks and I even heard that the Thames rose so high that it flowed into Westminster Hall."

"That was in October," Lord Wye said. "But no matter. Your orders are to push ahead as quickly as you can, Captain, keeping on every inch of sail possible. The Prime Minister expects me back in England in the quickest possible time."

"Very good, my Lord. But I warn you, if we run into one of these thunderstorms I have been hearing about in the town, it may be unpleasant. They say that they have had one or two of them lately, which sank several ships along the coast and on one occasion one of our troopships was so battered that they had to shoot a third of the horses."

Lord Wye was not interested, he had returned to the papers he was reading.

"With all possible speed, Captain," he said vaguely, his attention held by the letter he was reading.

"Very good, my Lord."

There was nothing for the Captain to do but leave the cabin.

As he closed the door behind him, Lord Wye looked up, a faint smile on his lips.

The Captain was getting old, he thought. He was over-cautious and afraid to take risks of any sort.

As far as he was concerned, he rather welcomed the storm. He was sick of soft living, of hanging around Carlton House and dancing attention on women. His eyes hardened as he thought of them.

There was Lady Bowhill, ready to throw herself into his arms and, although he had admired her beauty, he had imagined that she was virtuous and faithful to Sir Horace for whom he had a genuine regard.

Ah, well, women were the same everywhere. There had been that dark-eyed woman, rather pretty in a haggard way, who had flirted outrageously with him last night at the ball. Juanita something, he had forgotten her name.

But she was not the type that amused him and if he had not had a lot to drink he would not have cast her a second glance for all her manoeuvring and coquetry.

He threw down the papers and stretched his arms above his head. A storm might be quite a thrill.

And then his face darkened.

"Damn the Prime Minister for not letting me join the Armies," he swore aloud

Angrily he picked up a dispatch from the table. The Duke of Wellington had sent him a special note asking him to read the dispatches he had entrusted in his care and telling him privately of some of the difficulties that they were encountering.

> *"My men are in good health," he wrote, "but, although things have improved since I came out here, there are always difficulties in feeding an Army and those at home have no idea what it is to march for perhaps four days with nothing to eat. They talk about living off the country. Let them try it after six years of war and on the barren mountains, where even a goat cannot find enough to sustain it."*

Lord Wye rose to his feet.

Moving a little carefully, because he was too tall for the cabin and, on innumerable occasions, had knocked his head on the oak beams, he went to the porthole.

They had left the Harbour and were moving into the open sea. Lord Wye looked back and stared wistfully at the long line of barren mountains. If he had had wings, he would have flown towards them.

He wanted to see for himself what was happening beyond them. He wanted to smell gunpowder in his nostrils and the rough comradeship of men who were facing death or glory.

"Damn the Prime Minister!" he said again.

At that moment the cabin door opened.

"May I speak with you, my Lord?"

It was one of the junior Officers who spoke, a young man whom Lord Wye had chosen himself and he had a liking for him.

"Yes, Sanders, what is it?"

"It's a stowaway, my Lord. I thought you might like to know about it."

"A stowaway!"

"Yes, my Lord."

Lord Wye glanced out of the porthole to Lisbon, getting farther and farther away from them.

"Well, it's too late to send him back," he said. "Put him to work."

"That's just the difficulty, my Lord. And it's not a man, but a woman."

"A woman!"

Lord Wye was startled into expostulating the words quite loudly.

"Well, actually that is a slight exaggeration, my Lord. It is a child, a girl to be exact."

"Why on earth would a child want to stow away?" Lord Wye asked.

"I don't know, my Lord, I'm sure. But she is here and I thought that you would say what we are to do about her."

"What can we do?" Lord Wye enquired. "Bring her here to me. Can we understand anything she says?"

"I think so, my Lord."

"Bring her here," Lord Wye commanded.

"Very good, my Lord."

Sanders turned smartly about as Lord Wye settled himself once more in his high-backed chair.

The door opened a few moments later and a small figure was propelled somewhat forcibly into the cabin. The child, for at a glance it was obvious that she was nothing more, was cleanly but poorly dressed and, in Lord Wye's opinion, was quite obviously a Portuguese.

Her short dark hair fell lankly on either side of her small pointed face and her skin was very brown.

Only her eyes seemed unnaturally light and he noticed with some surprise that they were hazel-green, heavily fringed with dark lashes.

"Who are you?" he asked quietly. "Can you understand me?"

"Yes, indeed, my Lord. I speak English."

Her voice was low and, to his astonishment, cultured, although she had a faint accent.

"That is good. Now, suppose you tell me why you are here."

"I will tell you alone," the child said with some dignity. "I do not wish to speak in front of this man." She cast a disdainful glance at the blushing Sanders. "He has hurt my arm dragging me along the deck."

"She refused to come, my Lord," the young Officer piped up.

"That will be all, Sanders. I will talk to this young woman myself," Lord Wye said.

"Very good, my Lord."

Sanders went from the cabin, closing the door behind him. His attitude was that he obviously relinquished an unpleasant task with relief.

"Now you can tell your story," Lord Wye suggested. "Incidentally I should like the truth."

"Why should I tell you anything else?" the child asked.

She came a little nearer and now there was between them only the table where the dispatches lay. Lord Wye looked her up and down.

The girl was painfully thin and obviously undernourished.

He felt a sudden pity for all the inhabitants of the gallant little country that was fighting beside the English while all the rest of Europe was ground under the heel of Napoleon.

The ship lurched and she staggered.

Lord Wye then indicated a chair adjacent to his own.

"Will you not sit down?" he suggested.

"Thank you."

She had a strange dignity as well as grace, he thought. There must be some breeding somewhere.

"What is your name?" he asked.

"Elvina," she replied.

"That is your Christian name. Have you another?"

"It is of no consequence," she answered.

Lord Wye raised his eyebrows, but, as he made no comment, she continued almost as if she was repeating a well-learned lesson.

"My parents are dead. My sister is married to an Englishman and so I wish to reach England to be with her."

"An Englishman?" Lord Wye questioned. "What is his name?"

There was a little hesitation and then Elvina replied,

" – Thompson. Captain Thompson."

"He is in the Army then?"

"Yes."

"And he fought in Portugal? If he has gone home, I presume he was wounded?"

"Yes."

"And your sister returned with him?"

"Yes."

"It will be easy to trace him once we are in England," Lord Wye said.

"Then you will – take me?"

The question was quick and impulsive and there was a sudden light in those hazel-green eyes.

Lord Wye frowned.

"The whole thing is very unorthodox. You had no right to stow away on my yacht. Incidentally, how did you manage it? The guards must have been very lax."

Elvina smiled.

"I am very small," she replied. "They did not notice me."

Without thinking Lord Wye found himself smiling in return and then severely checked himself.

"It was extremely reprehensible," he said firmly. "In fact I am seriously annoyed at your trespass. Will there not be trouble at home? Will you not be missed? Will people not be searching for you?"

"Nobody cares – what happens to me," Elvina replied.

There was a little throb in her voice that told him this was the truth.

"If I did my duty," Lord Wye continued, "I would turn my yacht back or hail a passing ship bound for Lisbon and put you on it."

Elvina clasped her hands together.

"Please, my Lord, please take me to England. I am alone and terribly unhappy. In England it will be different. Please take me with you."

"And supposing we cannot find your sister?"

"We shall! I am sure we shall. Anyway – once I am there you need not worry about me. I can look after myself."

"I rather doubt that," Lord Wye replied. "You are only a child. You don't understand what it can be like to be alone and penniless in a strange country. Incidentally how old are you?"

There was a moment's hesitation before Elvina answered.

" – Thirteen, nearly fourteen."

Lord Wye nodded.

"That is what I thought. You are too young to have any idea of what you are doing. It is best that I send you back."

"No, no, please – don't! I beg of you! I pray – of you."

Elvina sprang to her feet and, coming round the side of the table, threw herself on her knees beside Lord Wye.

"Please, *please*, don't."

Her little face was turned up to his and there were tears in her eyes. He looked down at her for a moment.

"Very well," he then said. "But not out of consideration for your pleadings. Let me make that quite clear. Simply because it does not suit me at the moment to put back into Harbour or to waste time transferring you to another ship. I am in a hurry to return to England."

"I will be no trouble – I promise you."

"Women aboard are always a trouble," Lord Wye answered. "Have you brought any luggage with you?"

"Only a small bundle," Elvina answered.

"Well, that will have to suffice you for the voyage. And it is going to be rough. I hope you are a good sailor."

"I am never sick," Elvina replied. "I have been out in the fishing boats when they could scarcely bring them into Harbour and the seas have been so dangerous that even some of the older men have been seasick – but I have never even felt ill."

"Well, that is fortunate at any rate," Lord Wye said drily.

He walked across to the cabin door and opened it. As he expected, a sailor was in attendance outside.

"Prepare the next door cabin," Lord Wye ordered.

He turned round to look at the stowaway. She was seated again in the chair that she had vacated to fall at his knees. She was leaning back, relaxed, her hand resting elegantly on the arm.

Lord Wye noticed that she had long thin fingers. He saw too because her head was turned away from him that in profile her features were distinctly aristocratic.

He had a sudden qualm that he might be carrying away one of the Portuguese Nobility. A nice fool he would look if there was a hue and cry and it was discovered that the child belonged to some Nobleman who would accuse him of having kidnapped her.

"What is your surname?" he said, his voice almost harsh.

She looked up at him, her eyes wide.

"My mother is dead," she answered, "and so – so is – my father. I have no surname. I am not wanted. I belong to – nobody."

"That is not what I asked you," Lord Wye said. "Everyone has a name. Your sister must have had a name before she married Captain Thompson. What was it?"

"What does it matter?" Elvina enquired. "It will mean nothing to you. I promise you I am of no consequence. I see what you are thinking – you are wondering if there will be trouble if people will accuse you of taking me away with you. I swear to you there is nothing like that. I am nobody. Look at my clothes. Do I look rich – or grand? They are my own, I give you my oath on it."

"Why can you not answer my question in a straightforward manner?" Lord Wye asked.

"That is my business," Elvina said with a little toss of her head. "It's a lady's privilege to be unpredictable."

Lord Wye threw back his head and laughed.

The child was amusing, there was no doubt about that. She might look little better than a beggar, but she had certainly been educated.

"Would you tell me a little more about yourself?" he suggested. "As you see, I am asking you in all politeness."

"It's a boring subject that your Lordship will find little of interest in," Elvina replied. "Let me tell you other things instead. About the War, of the difficulties and discomforts your countrymen have suffered in this foreign land, of their victories – and their defeats. Is not that what you will be interested to hear?"

It was uncanny, Lord Wye thought, how this child seemed almost to read his thoughts. It would interest him.

"And what will you know about it?" he asked lightly. "At your age you should have been kept at home doing your lessons."

"I have walked about the streets and talked to the men resting between the battles," Elvina answered. "I have been to the hospitals and tried to help the wounded – when there were too many for the orderlies to cope with and not enough volunteers amongst the women of the town. I have heard the soldiers talk of their battles and have watched many of them die, speaking of the Duke of Wellington as if he was a kind of God who had led them to Heaven – instead of to death and destruction."

Lord Wye sat down suddenly in his chair.

"Go on talking," he urged her. "Tell me more."

*

Some hours later Elvina looked round the cabin that had been allotted her.

"You will be comfortable, it is the cabin that Lady Bowhill occupied on the way out," Lord Wye had said to her.

Elvina, seated on the edge of the bunk, decided that Lady Bowhill must be the woman who had tried to cling to Lord Wye last night and who had complained so passionately at his departure.

He was bored with her, she thought shrewdly.

Walking across the cabin with difficulty, because the ship was lurching in a most uncomfortable manner, she looked at herself in the looking glass that was fastened securely to the wall.

For a moment she thought that she must be crazy.

Last night in the cracked mirror in her own bedroom and in her hurry, it had been difficult to see the result of Juanita's dye and the walnut juice. But now her darkened face stared back at her and she was almost frightened by her own ugliness.

Her hair, which had waved naturally, hung straight and lank. The dye combined with the salty air had made it sticky. Elvina wondered what would happen if she washed it and then decided that it would be far too dangerous. She had applied the walnut juice to her face, neck, arms and legs well diluted, but, even so, it had made her skin very brown.

'It's not surprising that he believed I was Portuguese,' she told her reflection and made a resolution to remember to have a faint accent.

It had been easy enough to assume when Lord Wye was asking her questions, but when she grew animated she had suddenly become aware that her voice was clear and untrammelled by anything but animation.

"Why do you speak such good English?" Lord Wye had asked her.

"My parents had English friends in Lisbon," Elvina replied truthfully.

"And, of course, your sister married an Englishman," Lord Wye added.

"Yes, yes, of course."

Elvina now wished that she had not invented a mythical sister waiting for her in England and yet once she was aboard she had begun to think that she should have a reason for being so anxious to reach England.

It did not seem very reasonable for her to explain to Lord Wye that she was running away because of the cruelty of her stepmother and the drunkenness of her father.

Even if he believed her, he might still feel beholden to send her back to those who she rightfully belonged to.

It was when she was lying in the hold of the ship, having crept in under cover of the darkness and hidden herself behind some bales, that the weals from the whipping that Juanita had given her earlier in the day began to hurt unbearably.

There had been so much for her to do, first of all dressing Juanita and then going to watch the ball that she had not been concerned with the ache and the stiffness of her own body.

Alone in the darkness, the only sound the lap of the water against the sides of the yacht and the tramp of the armed guard overhead, she had thought that never again could she suffer die indignity and pain of being beaten by Juanita.

She tried to count up how many whippings she had endured and found it impossible to remember them.

There had been too many. Just as there had been too many slaps and pinches and screaming rages of abuse when Juanita cursed her and told her the day would come when she would cast her out and leave her to the mercy of the soldiers.

Elvina knew only too well what they meant. Men who had come out of battle or were just going into it, for that matter, wanted only two things – drink and women.

And once they had the drink it did not matter to them much what the women looked like. Young or old, so long as she was a woman they had a use for her.

'I have escaped! *I have escaped*!' Elvina told herself when morning came and she knew it by the sounds of activity on deck although there was no light in the hold.

She heard the anchor being weighed and the yacht began to move. She put her thin little arms round her body and hugged herself.

Her back might ache, she might be hungry and thirsty.

Nothing mattered except the fact that she was being carried away from Juanita, from Lisbon, from the misery of a house haunted by the ghost of her dead mother and the degradation of her seldom sober father.

She had not meant to come out from her hiding place for a long time, perhaps when they had been at sea for a day or more.

But two seamen surprised her and, although she had tried to escape from them, they had caught her.

'I am safe now,' Elvina told her reflection in the glass.

She wished that in her disguise she did not have to look so hideous. But once again her instinct had been right. As the English child of an English parent, Lord Wye would have taken her back to Lisbon.

She did not know why she had not invented a name for herself.

It seemed silly, but she did not wish to lie to Lord Wye any more than she was absolutely obliged to do. She had indeed kept as near to the truth as was possible in saying that nobody loved her and she was unwanted.

The mythical sister in England had been a necessity, so had the fact that her father was dead.

'He is dead as far as I am concerned,' Elvina justified herself. 'Half the time he is not aware of my existence and for the rest he believes what Juanita tells him. He died when my mother died and therefore I have no one, no one at all.'

There was a sudden hint of tears in her eyes and then she smiled.

'I am Elvina Nobody from Nowhere!' she told her reflection and suddenly she was laughing.

Laughing at the adventure of it all, at the excitement of being at sea and knowing that England lay ahead. England – and perhaps a chance of meeting her mother's relations.

She put out her hand and touched the locket. It was safe where she had put it, hidden between her breasts and she looked down at the ring on her little finger.

That was there too, her only two treasures, two things that had belonged to her mother. They were more valuable to her than all the wealth in King Joseph's baggage carts.

She jumped up suddenly, remembering why she had come to her cabin. The midday meal was to be served in a few minutes in Lord Wye's cabin.

She was to eat with him.

She washed her hands and face a little gingerly. She was half-afraid that the dye would come off in the basin. But she need not have been afraid, that stain was good and, when she combed back her hair from her forehead, it seemed to have a little more life in it

'I shall get quite used, in time to being a brunette' Elvina decided. 'And when we get to England, I can wash it away until I look like myself again.'

Over the round neck of her gown she put a clean white fichu, which made her skin seem in contrast darker than ever.

Then she went back to Lord Wye's cabin.

It seemed to Elvina that she had never had so much to eat before.

There were fresh lobsters, roast chicken, young mountain lamb, fruit and wine. There was also cheese made from goats' milk by the peasants, which Lord Wye declared that he found delicious.

"Do you eat like this – every day?" she asked.

He put out his hand impulsively and laid it on hers.

"You poor child," he said. "I am ashamed how we in England forget that you and your countrymen have suffered a great deal on our behalf. Perhaps by being kind to you, Elvina, I shall be able to pay back a little of the debt we all owe to Portugal."

His hand was strong and warm on hers and in response her eyes seemed to shine in her small pointed face.

"You are kind," she said. "I was sure of it when I heard you say – "

She stopped suddenly. She had been about to add – 'that you were sorry for the children last night' and realised that it would be a mistake.

Instead she substituted,

" – that you would take me to England."

"And when we get there I will find your sister. I promise you that," Lord Wye smiled, taking his hand away and pouring her out another glass of wine. "It should not be difficult to trace a Captain Thompson through the Army records. Do you like your brother-in-law?"

"Very – much," Elvina said a little stiffly.

Lord Wye was being frank and open with her and she hated having to lie to him.

"Tell me about yourself, my Lord," she said quickly. "What do you do?"

"I have a country estate in Hertfordshire," he answered, "and a house in London."

"You are married?"

Elvina was sure that he was not and yet she wanted to be quite certain. She was not sure why she was so interested.

"No, I have avoided that enviable state so far," Lord Wye responded with a smile.

It made it easier that he was a bachelor, Elvina thought. A married man might know more about women and might be more suspicious.

A plate on the end of the table leapt in the air and crashed to the floor.

"It is getting rough," Lord Wye said, as if they had not been pitching for several hours.

"Steward. Clear the table."

"Very good, my Lord."

The Steward took away what remained of the meal. There was no doubt at all that the sea was getting much rougher.

Now it was impossible to stand up. Everything moveable in the cabin had been fastened down.

The lanterns overhead swung dizzily backwards and forwards, creaking as they did so, and Elvina had to cling to her chair with both hands.

There was the sound of orders being given outside.

"What is happening?" Lord Wye asked the Steward.

"We are takin' down the mains'l, my Lord."

"That will slow us up," Lord Wye said angrily. "Tell the Captain to shorten it, but not to take it down completely."

"Very good, my Lord."

The Steward staggered from the cabin and Lord Wye settled himself in his chair.

"Frightened?" he asked.

Elvina shook her head.

"Why should I be? You are not afraid."

"Women usually are afraid of storms," Lord Wye replied. "But then you are not a woman, are you, Elvina?"

She smiled.

"If getting older is going to make me afraid of things like that, then I would rather remain as I am – "

" – a very naughty child!" Lord Wye finished, but his voice was not severe and his eyes were twinkling.

"Are you angry with me, my Lord?"

He almost believed that there was a hint of genuine apprehension in her voice and in the clearness of those strange hazel-green eyes.

"I ought to be," he answered. "I ought to be extremely incensed with you, first of all for invading my yacht and secondly for disturbing my privacy. I had looked forward to a quiet voyage with no one to talk to and no one to distract me. But shall I tell you the truth?"

"Yes, please do," Elvina said.

"I am damned if I don't enjoy having you here. I can hardly credit that I should want to talk to such an incalculable imp of mischief, but I do."

He smiled at her again.

Their eyes met and Elvina felt as if a sudden shaft of sunshine had come through the portholes to illuminate the cabin.

No one had ever been so kind to her before.

No one had ever told her, since her mother had died, that they wished to talk with her.

And then, as she looked at him, her heart beating a little quicker because of her happiness, the door was suddenly burst open and a gust of wind swept in almost like a tongue of fire.

"The Captain's compliments, my Lord," Mister. Sanders gasped. "We've got to take the mains'l down. The main mast is cracking!"

CHAPTER THREE

Afterwards Elvina could never remember in detail what had happened during the rest of that day and most of the night.

She could only recall being flung across the cabin so often that in the end she remained on the floor and even had difficulty in preventing herself from being rolled like a barrel to and fro with the movement of the yacht.

Outside there were hoarse shouts, the sudden shriek of a man in pain, the cracking and creaking of the ship's timbers which sounded at times as if the yacht itself was breaking in half.

Once Lord Wye came into the cabin to fetch a sling for a man who had broken his arm.

He snatched the first thing he saw, some small flags that had fallen from the drawer and which were lying all over the floor with a miscellaneous collection of other objects.

He was soaked to the skin and looked very different from the dandified gentleman who had left the cabin some hours earlier.

"What is – happening?" Elvina asked him.

"We are still afloat," he answered with a smile, his teeth were very white in contrast to his face that had been whipped by the wind and rain.

"Are we in – danger, my Lord?"

"Perhaps," he replied. "But we shall survive. The yacht is well built."

He held onto the table to prevent himself from toppling over.

"Are you all right?" he asked.

Elvina nodded,

"It's better to lie on the floor than be thrown onto it."

"You have more common sense than most people," he smiled. "Don't be afraid. This damned wind must abate some time."

It seemed doubtful, Elvina thought, hearing the shrieking fury of it, swirling around the yacht, so that she realised that she and Lord Wye were shouting at each other.

"You are wet," she exclaimed. "Have you no coat?"

"I have not time to put one on," he answered.

She realised that in some strange way he was enjoying the battle with the elements, the feeling that he was pitting his strength and that of his yacht against nature itself.

"Is the mast all right?" she shouted.

"I think it will hold," he replied. "And if the worst comes to the worst, we shall be picked up by one of the English ships. There are plenty of them in the Bay if we could but see them. When this blinding rain clears, we shall be able to send a signal for help."

His words made Elvina realise how serious their plight was. But before she could question him further, he had gone. She was left alone in the dishevelled cabin.

Hours went by. Everything that could fall onto the floor had fallen, everything that could break had broken.

Elvina wedged herself against the leg of the table and clung to it. She could see and hear the waves through the porthole and it seemed to her that they must be breaking over the whole ship.

Some time during the afternoon there was a tremendous crash. It was like a cannon shot and she knew that the mast had gone.

She heard it fall upon the deck and was aware by the sudden list of the whole ship that the sails were dragging them to starboard. She could hear the men being ordered to cut them loose and she longed to go to the door and she what was happening.

She had, however, been to sea too often in her life not to know that, when anything went wrong, a woman on board was a nuisance and an encumbrance.

Besides she was well aware that it would not take much strength of wind or wave to sweep her overboard. She did not need to be instructed to stay where she was.

She knew instinctively that it was the thing she must do and so, despite her curiosity, she went on clinging to the fat carved leg of the oak table, which was battened securely to the floor, while she listened to what was occurring outside.

A little later she realised that they were free of the sails. The mast had been chopped off and thrown overboard. Now they were drifting with the wind at the mercy of the tempest.

Strangely enough Elvina was not afraid.

She had been, desperately tremblingly afraid of Juanita, especially when she held a whip in her hand, but the fury of the elements was something that had never frightened her.

It did cross her mind that they might be drowned, but somehow it did not seem to matter.

'If I die,' she thought, 'I shall be with Mama. If I live, I shall not have to go back to face Juanita and her beatings.'

In the next few hours she slept a little, still clinging by instinct to the table leg and it was with a start that she heard the cabin door open.

She felt the sudden gust of cold wind sweep around the cabin and realised that Lord Wye was visiting her once more.

He was wearing an oilskin now, a rough, coarsely cut one such as seamen wore, but the water was seeping from his clothes and running down over his boots making pools of water on the floor as he walked across it.

He reached for the edge of the table and guided himself to a chair.

"Are you all right?" he asked Elvina.

She looked up at him and gave a little cry. His face was smeared with blood where, on one side of his forehead, there was a huge gash.

"You are – hurt!" she exclaimed.

He put his fingers up to his face and then regarded them ruefully.

"A splinter from the mast caught me," he said. "It is nothing."

"I will bandage it for you."

"It does not matter," he answered. "There are three of my men with broken arms and one with a broken leg. We have also lost a man overboard."

There was no elation in his voice now and Elvina said gently,

"I heard – the mast go."

"Yes, it has gone and we are drifting helplessly. It is too rough to get the oars out. In fact there is nothing we can do until the rain clears."

"Are we well away from the coast?" Elvina enquired.

"God knows! The maps and papers went overboard and we have little left but our bump of location."

Elvina put up her hand and touched his knee.

"These storms do not last long."

"What do you call long?" Lord Wye asked sharply.

"Five or six hours is about the usual length. There were some last summer that raged longer, but they were exceptional."

"This one is quite exceptional enough for me," Lord Wye said grimly.

"Perhaps we could put in at Corunna," Elvina suggested.

"According to the Captain's calculations we should be past Corunna by now. With this wind behind us God knows how many knots we have been making since we left Lisbon."

Elvina said nothing more. She had no further suggestions to make.

Then a little timidly she asked,

"May I bandage your head – for you?"

Lord Wye put his head back against his chair and closed his eyes.

"If you wish."

She realised that he was utterly and completely exhausted. She had seen men like this once before when they had been battling with a storm at sea.

She had been down at the Harbour when a fishing boat was brought in almost broken into pieces and yet still afloat and the men had dragged it up the shingle to safety and then had flung themselves down on the stones and fallen asleep.

She could remember her surprise and then her understanding of the ordeal that they had been through and what it must have taken out of them.

Those had been rough strong men used to battling with the sea day after day and year after year.

If they had succumbed to fatigue, how much more so would it affect Lord Wye, who was not used to such exertions?

With difficulty she managed to cross the cabin and look amongst the mêlée of stuff spilled from the drawers for a bandage of some sort.

Finally she found her way through another door to a cabin, which she guessed was Lord Wye's. It was in a fantastic state of disarray. Everything was on the floor.

A mirror that had hung on the wall was smashed and a chair was overturned. Even the bedding had fallen from the bed.

By groping on her hands and knees Elvina managed to find some soft muslin cravats. There were also some fine linen handkerchiefs and soaking one in water, she crawled back to Lord Wye's side.

Holding onto his chair to steady herself, she swabbed the blood from his forehead and his face.

It was a bad gash, she perceived, with jagged edges and the flesh already looked purple and inflamed.

She remembered that her mother had always said that water, unless it had been boiled, might be dangerous to wounds and so bravely she started across the room again to a cupboard where she had seen the Steward place the bottle of wine after their meal was finished.

There was little of it left. It too was broken and, when she opened the cupboard door the wine poured out like a flow of blood.

She dipped the handkerchief in it and carrying it back to her patient dabbed it against the wound.

He stirred a little as if it stung him, but he did not wake.

Now with great difficulty Elvina managed to put a pad of clean linen against the wound and bind it with the muslin cravat.

It was not a job that she was particularly proud of, but at least it stopped the blood from flowing and it would keep the wound clean.

Then she went back to her place at the table leg, only glancing up above her every now and then to see that Lord Wye was comfortable and not in danger of being thrown from the chair.

With his legs stretched out in front of him, his wet clothes dripping until there was a pool of water around the chair, he looked the very picture of exhaustion.

He must have been working as one of the seamen himself, Elvina thought, because she could see that his fingernails were broken and his hands black with tar as if he had been pulling at a rope.

She wished that she could force him to change his clothes into something dry, but she knew it was almost impossible to waken him now.

He was deeply asleep, snoring a little as a man will who sleeps in an uncomfortable position.

He looked younger in repose, she thought, and far less awe-inspiring than he had done when she had first faced him across the table and answered his questions.

She realised now that she had been afraid, not only of him but most of all of being sent back.

She had escaped and she thought now that, if Lord Wye had insisted on taking her home, she might, in desperation, have jumped overboard.

But he had not refused her sanctuary.

She felt her heart soften and warm at the thought of his kindness.

Other men might have behaved quite differently.

Elvina had been brought up in a town continually full of soldiers and she was well aware of what might have happened to her had Lord Wye sent her forward with the seamen. That must indeed have seemed to him her rightful place.

A peasant child from Portugal, a shabby little stowaway, parentless and without a name!

Why should he have troubled himself, as he had done, to give her a cabin that was kept for his own guests, to let her eat with him and to treat her as if she was his equal?

Elvina gave a little sigh.

"Thank you!" she whispered aloud to the sleeping man. "Thank you for being – a great gentleman."

She remembered last night how his voice had softened when he had spoken of the children on the quay looking like skeletons.

It was those few words and the kindness she had sensed in him which had given her the idea of stowing away on his yacht, of throwing herself on his mercy and of travelling with him to England.

It had been a desperate and mad thing to do and yet her instinct had not been at fault. She had trusted a man and he had not been found wanting.

"Thank you," she said again and, putting out her hand, very gently touched his.

He was cold. Crawling across the cabin once more, she brought back a blanket from his bunk.

And yet, what use was a blanket when he was so wet? Elvina wondered if she could possibly try to undress him, as she had often tried to undress her father when he was too drunk to do it himself.

But she knew that such action would be impossible as far as Lord Wye was concerned.

It was not only because he was such a large man, six feet at least in height, it was because with the yacht still rolling it was impossible to keep one's balance even for a moment.

There was nothing she could do but put the blanket over him. She covered him up to his chin and tucked it round him in the chair.

He looked strange with his bandaged head emerging from a cocoon of soft white wool. But still he slept.

Elvina fetched another blanket for herself, draped it over her shoulders and cuddled down into the warmth of it. She had not realised until she thought of Lord Wye just how cold she was.

Her thin shawl was no protection against the wind that seemed to creep in even though the doors and portholes were barred against it.

Now it was growing dark outside and as the ship rose on the waves she could see a little glimpse of the sky.

It had been grey with the lashing rain, but now it was darkening into sable and Elvina was sure that it was not as rough as it had been.

The thunder, which had growled and grumbled overhead all the afternoon, was going farther away and although the rain still fell, even that was not so violent as it had been.

It was quieter too outside the cabin. But that meant nothing for without a sail they were helpless.

As Lord Wye had said, there was nothing they could do except to drift until the sea went down.

Now that the blanket was around her, Elvina felt a sense of comfort. She was sure that Lord Wye was more comfortable as well.

Wet though he might be, the blanket was engendering some heat and his expression was certainly that of a man at peace.

Elvina felt her eyelids dropping and the cabin was darkening. She slipped a little lower down onto the floor and she slept.

*

She awoke with a sudden start, wondering for a moment where she was and filled with a fear that she would feel Juanita's whip across her shoulders. And then she remembered that she had escaped.

She knew in an instant what had awakened her. Someone had come into the cabin and from her position beneath the table she could see his boots, high fisherman's boots, and she realised that why she could see them was because he held a lantern in his hand.

She moved as the light fell on her face and she looked up to see Mister Sanders standing there, his face very white in the candlelight with great dark lines of sleeplessness and exhaustion under his eyes.

Suddenly Elvina was aware that the yacht was no longer moving. There was the slap of the waves against the sides and there was the sound of the wind, a very much lower and gentler wind.

But they were not moving.

That was why Mister Sander's legs had seemed strange. That was why the lantern in its steadiness had seemed so surprising.

"What it? Where are we?" Elvina asked.

In answer Mister Sanders raised the lantern so that he could look at Lord Wye, still asleep beneath the confining warmth of the blanket.

"Don't waken him," Elvina cried. "He is tired, dead tired, leave him alone."

The young Officer looked down in surprise at the fierceness of her tone.

"He worked as hard as anyone," he said with a note of admiration in his voice. "If it had not been for him, the mast would have gone hours earlier than it did. He helped us lash it with ropes, but it was no use. It broke in the end."

"I heard it," Elvina said.

"It knocked a man overboard," Mister Sanders told her. "He had no hope in a sea like this."

"What is happening – now?"

"We are aground. That is what I have come to tell his Lordship."

"Where?"

Mister Sanders shrugged his shoulders.

"I have no idea. A sandbank of some sort. We shall know in an hour when it is light. The Captain thought he ought to know."

He nodded towards Lord Wye.

"Tell the Captain that his Lordship is asleep," Elvina said. "There is nothing he can do about it, is there?"

"There is nothing any of us can do," Mister Sanders answered. "Except pray that there is a British ship within hail. We have been trying to signal as it is."

"What about the enemy?" Elvina asked.

"You need not be afraid of them," Mister Sanders said scornfully. "Britain has command of the sea. Why, coming out here the place was like a regatta, British ships wherever you looked. Boney may have an Army, but he has no Navy. Nelson saw to that."

"But if we are stuck on a sandbank, we must be near the shore," Elvina commented.

"The Captain thinks we must have rounded Cape Finisterre by now," Mister Sanders said. "But personally I have my doubts. We might have been going North, East or West in that storm. Much more likely to land up in Oporto than anywhere else."

"No, no! We must be farther than that."

If they had only reached Oporto, Elvina knew only too well what would happen. Lord Wye would have second thoughts.

He would send her back to Lisbon. There would be a fishing boat or a transport of some sort. He might even try to send her overland. It would only be a question of paying to get someone to take her home by mule cart.

"I'll tell the Captain his Lordship is asleep," Mister Sanders said.

When he had gone from the cabin, Elvina got onto her knees and prayed,

'Please, God, don't let it be Oporto. Please, God, let it be further up the coast than that.'

She scrambled to her feet and went to the porthole, but nothing could be seen.

It was still dark and still raining, but now it was gentle ordinary rain and not the lashing, blinding sort that had battered against the porthole during the violent storm.

Elvina went to her own cabin, washed her face in cold water and, feeling in the confusion and mess on the floor, tried to find a comb for her hair.

She was unsuccessful and, thinking that she might find someone to light a lantern, she opened the door onto the deck.

Outside two or three lanterns had already been lit. One was placed over the entrance to the cabins and two others were suspended from what remained of the main mast.

Never had she seen such a scene of confusion. Everything was broken, battered and stained with seawater.

Two seamen were vainly trying to tidy things up, moving pieces of barrels that had smashed into a hundred pieces, coiling a tangle of ropes and pulling out the splinters of wood that had embedded themselves deeply in the deck.

On the bridge she could see the Captain talking to Mister Sanders and another Officer.

"'Tis no use guessing, Sanders," she heard the Captain say sharply. "I'll be honest and say I have not the slightest idea where we are."

"We shall know soon, sir."

The Captain looked up at the sky, the rain falling on his tired face.

"I suppose so. Let's hope it's a pleasant surprise."

"Shall I send out more signals, sir?" Mister Sanders asked.

The Captain debated for a moment.

"I suppose so. But keep them out to sea. God knows what we shall find on the land, if there is land to starboard."

Someone on the deck caught sight of Elvina standing at the cabin door.

"Is there anything you want, miss?" a seaman asked.

"I should like a lantern, if you please," Elvina answered.

"Good Lord! I had forgotten our stowaway," she heard the Captain say. "Is she all right?"

"Quite all right, sir," Mister Sanders answered. "Give the child some food, she must be famished. And I daresay his Lordship will want something to eat when he wakes."

"I think we could all do with a meal," Mister Sanders said. "I know I feel as if I could eat a whole roasted ox."

"Go and see to it then," the Captain remarked wearily.

A seaman carried one of the lanterns into Elvina's cabin and kindled a light in the one that hung there. He also went into the main cabin and lit the lanterns above the table while Lord Wye still slept

Elvina tidied herself as best she could and, covering her shoulders with her shawl for the dawn wind was chilly, she went back into the main cabin.

It was not until the Steward brought slices of ham and cold chicken on a broken plate that Lord Wye opened his eyes.

For a moment he struggled against the confining blanket and then sat up.

"What the devil – ?" he began.

Then he saw Elvina.

"So, we are alive!" he exclaimed. "Have I been asleep for long?"

"Not very long, my Lord," she answered.

"What is happening? Why have we stopped?"

"The ship is aground," she told him.

"The devil it is!"

He sprang to his feet, crossed the cabin and disappeared. She gave a little sigh and with difficulty restrained herself from taking one of the pieces of ham and eating it in her fingers.

The Steward came back with bread baked the day before in Lisbon, butter and some pewter mugs.

"All the china is broken," he said with a smile. "But there are some bottles of ale intact, unless his Lordship would rather have something stronger for breakfast."

"I should think his Lordship will be grateful for anything," Elvina answered.

"That goes for all of us," the Steward added. "The sea has got into the meat and most of the water barrels are damaged. But we'll be able to get some more now that we'll have to put into Port."

"Where are we likely – to do that?" Elvina asked.

The Steward shrugged his shoulders.

"The Captain was talking of Corunna or we might have to go back to Oporto. There's a better Harbour there."

Elvina drew a deep breath.

Lord Wye came stumping back into the cabin.

"Heaven knows where we are. I will have something to eat, change my clothes and by that time it should be dawn."

"There is only ale to drink, unless you would like – something stronger," Elvina said.

"Ale will do me," Lord Wye replied. "But what about you?"

"I will have a little ale too," Elvina said with a smile.

"Are you hungry?" Lord Wye asked.

"Very," she replied.

"You are a funny little thing," he said, settling himself at the table. "Most children of your age would have been screaming themselves silly at a storm like that. You were as good as gold and, what is more, I find that you have bandaged my head. I told you not to worry."

"You have a nasty gash there," Elvina said. "It will take some time before it knits. Does it hurt?"

"It throbs a bit, but I am more concerned about the men below decks. We do not carry a doctor in a ship of this size, but the Captain has some knowledge of setting bones. He is going to see what he can do when he has time."

"I wish I could help," Elvina declared.

Lord Wye stared at her.

"You?" he asked. "Goodness, that is not woman's work."

"In the hospitals the orderlies were usually drunk," Elvina said. "That was why the nuns used to go and nurse the soldiers. They were really wonderful."

"I have heard that. I only hope, if I am ever wounded, that I shall have a nun to look after me. Or you. You are nearly as good as one, aren't you?"

He was joking, but Elvina answered seriously.

"Please let me bandage your head again now that the ship is steady. It was not easy to do when I had to hold onto the chair with one hand."

"Eat your breakfast and then you can do as you like," Lord Wye said.

"You will change. Promise me that you will change your clothes."

He looked at her with a little twist of his lips.

"I thought I had got myself a stowaway. But it seems she is a nurse."

"All men need one," Elvina said, smiling at him.

"Don't believe it," Lord Wye replied. "What most men want is to get away from women of all sorts and every sort.

That is why they go to sea. It is the one place women cannot drop in on you. Unless, of course, they stow away."

"I am sorry if I spoiled your plans for the journey home," Elvina said. "I have not brought you much luck, have I? Now we shall be delayed."

"I am afraid so. It means having a new mast fitted. That may take time. I shall have to pick up an English ship."

Elvina stopped eating and put her hands to her heart

"Does that mean – you would leave me behind?" she asked.

"Well, if we are off the coast of Portugal, as I suspect, you could always go home."

"No! *No!*"

It was a cry of sheer terror.

"I cannot do that. Do you not understand? I cannot."

"But you must have lived somewhere before you came aboard my yacht," Lord Wye said. "You have been very mysterious about it, but someone must have looked after you. Was it the nuns in a Convent?"

"No, my Lord, I swear to you that I have not run away from a Convent or a school. I cannot go back to where I was living. It would be impossible. They would beat me unmercifully if they knew that I had tried to escape."

Lord Wye helped himself to another piece of ham.

"You know I am beginning to think you exaggerate. It is a prerogative of your sex, of course. But I don't believe that young women are beaten for no particular reason."

"You don't believe it," Elvina said rising to her feet and facing him across the table. "Then look for yourself. See just some of the marks on my body."

She pulled the fichu from her neck as she spoke and shrugged one shoulder free of her shabby cotton gown.

Then she turned her back on him.

Only one shoulder was revealed, but that was criss-crossed with a dozen weals from Juanita's whip. Crimson, where the blood had broken on some of them, the rest were turning all colours of the rainbow, purple, black, blue and orange.

They made Elvina's back look like some distorted pattern made by an artist crazy in the use of his paints.

"*Good God!*"

There was no mistaking the surprise and horror in Lord Wye's voice.

Elvina pulled her gown on again and turned to face him, putting the white fichu around her neck.

"Now do you understand?" she asked.

"Who has done this to you? Who has dared to treat you like that?" he asked.

"Just the woman who was looking after me since my mother died."

"She must be a fiend," Lord Wye expostulated.

"Some people find her attractive," Elvina remarked with a little smile at the corner of her mouth.

"I did not believe that such women existed," Lord Wye answered.

"You will not leave me – behind?" Elvina said in a very small voice.

"I don't know what you are letting me in for," Lord Wye grunted.

"Promise me, *please* promise me," Elvina said. "If you go home in a British ship, take me with you."

"Well, it will be a bit embarrassing to arrive on board with a Portuguese stowaway. What do you imagine people are going to think? You may be a child, but you are a female one."

"You cannot leave me behind," Elvina besought him. "I will do anything, anything you suggest, if only you will take me with you."

"I am not sure it will be possible. You must be reasonable about this."

"You can make it possible." Elvina said. "You can do anything. You are rich and important. People listen to you."

"We will have to see. That is all I have to say. If the worst comes to the worst, I suppose you could come back with the yacht. It will be repaired some time."

Even as he spoke he met Elvina's eyes across the table and knew what she was thinking.

"I can trust the Captain," he said. "He is a decent man with a family of his own."

"I want to go with – you."

"I can only hope it will be possible," Lord Wye replied. "It is no use forcing me to promise things that I cannot perform."

"Promise me you will try to take me with you," Elvina said. "Promise that at any rate."

He stared at her for a moment in exasperation.

"*Dammit*," he muttered. "Can a man not even have his breakfast without a woman nagging at him?"

Then suddenly he smiled.

"All right, you tiresome little imp, I will give you my word. Anything for peace and quiet."

Elvina's eyes shone like stars across the table.

"Thank you," she cried. "Thank you. *Thank you*. I know that you will not go back on your promise."

"I will bet a monkey that you will not let me. Now for Heaven's sake stop talking and let me think what we have to do. It's not going to be easy to get out of the mess we are in now. It is getting lighter. So let's go and see what can be done."

"But you have not changed," Elvina cried.

"I have no time now."

He lifted the pewter mug to his lips and then, getting to his feet, went towards the door.

"Come back quickly," Elvina said. "I have to bandage your head. You said I could."

He did not answer, but she knew that he had heard her for he turned to smile at her before he reached the door.

As he did so, there came a sudden knock and the door opened inwards.

"The Captain's compliments, my Lord. There's a ship approaching."

"It sounds as if our signals got through," Lord Wye commented.

"It's from the starboard side, my Lord."

"The devil it is!"

Lord Wye went from the cabin and Elvina sprang to her feet and ran after him.

Sure enough from the starboard side of the ship, coming through the hazy grey mist, was the faint silhouette of a large ship manned by some twenty oars.

Everyone had crowded up on deck, even the men with their broken arms in slings. They all stood waiting, and Elvina, watching from the doorway of the cabin, felt that every man held his breath.

And then an order came ringing across the space between the ships. An order given by a man they could vaguely discern, standing in the bow.

And with a sudden feeling of horror that was almost like a stab in her heart Elvina realised that he spoke in French!

CHAPTER FOUR

The very second after Lord Wye heard the French words coming through the grey mist, he turned and ran as quickly as he could into the cabin, brushing past Elvina at the door.

She stared at him in amazement

For one incredible moment she thought that he was running away and then she realised that he was snatching up the dispatches that had lain on the table, but had been thrown by the storm into every corner of the cabin.

There were some things he threw down again, having glanced at them, others he held tightly in his hand, looking round desperately as if he debated where to put them.

"Let me take them."

Elvina spoke without thinking. She only knew that because she understood his perplexity, she must help.

Without argument Lord Wye passed her two closely folded dispatches.

She thrust them down the front of her shabby gown and then felt his hand on her shoulder.

His touch meant comfort, encouragement and thanks and then, still without words, he brushed past her and was out again on the deck.

It had all taken such an incredibly short time that the ship approaching them seemed little nearer than if had when they first realised what it contained.

The other occupants of the yacht stood staring into the mist.

Only the Captain was vocal about the danger that threatened them.

"'Tis the blood-stained Frenchies, blast them!" he cried "Can we hold them off, my Lord?"

It was a despairing question and an effort at defiance that would have been doomed from the very outset.

For now, as the boat drew nearer, they could see that the man in the bow had been joined by half a dozen others all with their muskets levelled at the yacht.

"We can do nothing," Lord Wye replied. "It is death to all of us if we make a move. Keep calm and leave this to me."

A voice, speaking in French, seemed almost unnaturally loud.

"Who are you?" it asked.

"We are the yacht *Fontaine*, a private vessel that has suffered by the storm," Lord Wye answered, also speaking French, but with a pronounced English accent. "Our mast is broken and we are stuck on a sandbank."

"In the name of the Emperor Napoleon Bonaparte we are about to board you," was the reply.

Elvina saw the despair on the faces of the seamen standing around.

She knew that Lord Wye was right. To try to oppose this boat full of armed men was to commit suicide. As it was, they were left with only half their original crew. The rest were injured and below deck.

She heard the Captain cursing beneath his breath and wondered how Lord Wye could appear so calm.

With his bandaged head, his crumpled damp garments and his sailor's oilskin, he certainly did not look a dandy.

Yet she felt that anyone, even a Frenchman, could not help but recognise that he was of noble birth.

They could hear it in his unhurried speech, see it in his air of authority as he waited calmly and without any expression of fear or agitation until the Officer commanding the ship stepped aboard.

Then with courtesy he stepped forward to meet him.

"You are the owner of this yacht?"

The question was sharp and the voice aggressive.

"Allow me to present myself," Lord Wye replied. "I am Lord Wye of the Royal Household of His Majesty King George the Third of England."

"You must consider yourself my prisoner, my Lord," the Frenchman replied.

Short, stout and very conscious of his own importance, he was obviously impressed by Lord Wye's status for his tone was now less arrogant and offensive.

"I am afraid there is nothing else I can do," Lord Wye answered, "except to hope that you will be able to salvage my yacht. It is extremely valuable and it would be a pity if she should go to the bottom."

"Valuable? What are you carrying?" the Frenchman enquired suspiciously.

"Quite a number of things that might be of interest to you," Lord Wye replied. "Will you come to the cabin and perhaps we can discuss it over a glass of wine."

Elvina, listening, stared in amazement.

The last thing she had expected was that Lord Wye would speak so politely or indeed so graciously to the enemy.

She was used to hearing soldiers' tales of the brutal manner in which the French treated their prisoners, especially the Portuguese and Spaniards, and she had no idea that there was anything one could do as regards Frenchmen except try to kill them.

But here was Lord Wye, whom she knew to be a patriot, speaking in a most genial manner as if he was inviting an old friend to drink with him.

It was utterly bewildering and even more so when, having given orders to his men to board and search the yacht, the French Officer followed Lord Wye into the cabin where two seamen were instructed to tidy things up and bring both food and wine.

Elvina herself shrank back into the shadows cast by the lanterns, but the very instant he entered the Frenchman saw her.

"Who is this?" he demanded.

There was just a moment's hesitation before Lord Wye replied fluently, but with his execrable accent,

"*Ma fille!* Elvina, let me present the Commodore of the boarding party. I am afraid, *monsieur*, I did not hear your name."

"Bouvais," the Frenchman replied. "Pierre Bouvais."

Elvina dropped him a curtsey, only a small one. It went against the grain that she must bend her knee to the enemy.

But she sensed that Lord Wye was playing some subtle game and she knew that she must do her part. What was more, he obviously expected it of her.

"Your daughter?" Monsieur Bouvais queried.

Elvina realised with a little inward smile that it must seem strange that a fair tall Englishman should produce a black-haired, dark-skinned child and claim her as his own.

"My wife is Portuguese," Lord Wye explained airily. "I was visiting her in Lisbon. I am afraid the War you are waging, *monsieur*, has not until now concerned me very closely. I am so occupied in obeying His Majesty's commands that I have no time for fighting."

"And yet you have been to Lisbon," the Commodore replied, his eyes narrowing. "There are many troops landing at Lisbon I hear."

"I was on a more amicable mission," Lord Wye replied. "It was to visit my wife. As you see, she has sent back with me my eldest child so that the journey to England should not seem too long or too tedious. Will you not be seated, *monsieur*?"

The Frenchman glanced at Elvina again as if he did not believe what he had heard.

By now the Stewards had cleared the floor and Elvina noticed with relief that, in taking away the broken pieces of glass, china and other things that had fallen from the drawers, they had also taken the rest of the dispatches that Lord Wye had not considered of such import that they necessitated concealment.

She could hear the ones he had given her crackling a little as she moved and the edge of the paper was sharp against her skin.

"Come and sit down, Elvina," Lord Wye suggested. "We must tell Monsieur Bouvais about the storm last night. We must convince him of how bad it was or I am afraid he will think our navigation was at fault that we should find ourselves in such a predicament. By the way, *monsieur*, where are we?"

"You are just outside the harbour of St. Jean de Luz," the Commodore replied. "We saw your signals and wondered what they could be. But I suppose you realise that you must have missed the cliffs by a very narrow margin. The sandbanks only start at the entrance to the Harbour."

"I suppose that we should be grateful that we were not battered to death," Lord Wye said. "I am wondering, however, if a French prison would be preferable."

"We will, of course, do our best to make your Lordship comfortable," the Frenchman said with a sarcastic twist of his lips.

Elvina clenched her fists together under the table. She hated the Frenchman and yet she realised that to be antagonistic and rude might only make things worse.

A prisoner of the French! She had never dreamed of such a fate, not even when Napoleon's Armies had defeated the expeditionary force under Sir John Moore.

Always at Lisbon they had seemed safe. And now to escape from Juanita for this! She felt her lips go dry at the thought of what lay ahead.

Yet still Lord Wye was going out of his way to be charming.

"Ah, here is the wine," he said as the Steward approached with a miraculously unbroken decanter and two glasses. "I did not believe that there was anything on board that had not been smashed to bits. Surely you are fortunate."

The Frenchman took a drink. A French seaman entered and without apology marched up to him and, leaning over, spoke in his ear.

Elvina could not hear what he said, but it was obviously satisfactory for Monsieur Bouvais smiled.

"*Bon!*" he said. "*Très bon!*"

The seaman saluted and left and Monsieur Bouvais smiled his mocking sarcastic smile at Lord Wye.

"I see you have not misinformed me. The yacht is indeed a privately owned vessel and very comfortably fitted out.

You have good stores on board. What would you say was the value of this vessel?"

Lord Wye shrugged his shoulders.

"It cost me five thousand pounds to build," he replied. "I have spent another two or three thousand pounds on her since."

He waited a moment to let his words sink in and then added,

"You have captured a prize, *monsieur*. I hope you will get your share of what it is worth."

The Frenchman's eyes narrowed.

"It may not be possible to tow her in."

"I should think it quite possible with your particular ship," Lord Wye contradicted him. "Of course my men would be prepared to help you. In England salvage money is always divided between those who do the work. It would be a pity on this occasion if your share was diminished unnecessarily."

The Frenchman drummed with his fingers on the table.

"It will be a long job," he said reflectively. "The tide has only just gone out. The sandbank will not be covered again until late this afternoon."

"What is the hurry?" Lord Wye asked. "I assure you, my dear *monsieur*, that I have no anxiety to see the inside of my quarters in St. Jean de Luz."

"Your men would help us?" the Frenchman asked.

"Those of them who have not suffered from the storm," Lord Wye answered. "For the others I would ask your clemency."

"I am not certain that it is possible," the Frenchman said quickly. "If we were to signal to the shore they would send out other ships."

"The salvage money would then be sadly depleted," Lord Wye pointed out. "And apart from the value of the yacht itself, there is not a great deal on board. Some wine, if it is not broken and the furnishings of the cabins. That is all. It is the yacht herself that is valuable."

"Yes, yes, I see," Monsieur Bouvais nodded. "I was just wondering if we could do it."

"Supposing you have a talk with my Captain, when, of course, you have finished your meal," Lord Wye suggested. "You will permit me to have a word with him myself?"

He rose and walked to the window.

"The sun is rising. You will have to make up your mind, *monsieur.*"

"Have the Captain brought here," the Commodore snapped to a French seaman waiting in the doorway, a musket on his shoulder.

Elvina listened, but she did not understand what was happening.

She was well aware that Lord Wye had some plan, but she must wait for it to unfold, afraid in the meantime of doing something wrong.

The Captain was brought to the cabin, his arms had been bound behind him and there was a sullen look of resignment on his face.

Elvina caught the glance that passed between him and Lord Wye over the Frenchman's head. Wordlessly Lord Wye had signalled something that the Captain understood.

He agreed wholeheartedly that his men should help the French vessel tow the yacht into Harbour.

"What time is full tide?" the Captain asked in English and Lord Wye translated it for him.

"About six o'clock, perhaps a little later," the Frenchman replied.

"If we start to get her off then and take her slowly, there should be no mishaps," Lord Wye said. "In the meantime my men can make any repairs that may be necessary. They have already reported a small leak in the bow."

"I can have it done immediately," the Captain volunteered.

"Perhaps, *monsieur*, you would deem it possible to release the Captain," Lord Wye suggested gently. "And if the other men aboard are in irons, it would be a wise move to set them free. The sooner they get to work the better."

"Yes, yes," the Frenchman agreed and gave the order.

"And now another glass of wine, *monsieur*?" Lord Wye invited him. "I have a claret below that I should very much appreciate your opinion on. After all it comes from your country and I have been told it is the best the Bordeaux valley can produce, but I should value a connoisseur's opinion on that."

The Steward brought more wine and the Frenchman became more genial.

The sun was rising and Elvina had a great desire to see what lay outside.

"Might I go and tidy myself?" she asked Lord Wye, wondering if she should add 'Papa' to her plea, but feeling that would be embarrassing.

"I am sure Monsieur Bouvais will be only too pleased to let you go to your cabin, my dear," Lord Wye replied in quite a paternal manner. "Perhaps it would be wise for you to have a little rest. You passed a sleepless night I am afraid."

"She can go," the Frenchman said, raising his glass once more to his lips.

"Thank you, *monsieur*."

Elvina curtseyed and went towards her cabin.

Once inside she did not worry about her appearance, but ran to the porthole.

It had stopped raining and the sun was shining hazily on the narrow strip of sea that lay between them and the small red-roofed town. There were only a few houses and the pointed spire of a Church.

"My first visit to France!"

Elvina said the words aloud despairingly and yet she knew that if they had come ashore South of St. Jean de Luz it would not have helped them much.

San Sebastián was in the hands of the French, as was most of the Northern coast of Spain. They were prisoners, captured and with no chance of escape, and now the full horror of it swept over her so that she put her hands to her eyes and felt herself shiver.

Napoleon Bonaparte had been the bogey of Europe for so long that she had grown up with tales of horror and terror, really believing all Frenchmen to be inhuman brutal monsters that no one could trust, least of all a woman.

She was well aware why Lord Wye had introduced her as his daughter. She knew too, if the stories that were circulated in Lisbon were to be believed, that her youth would not save her.

It had not saved the children in the parts of Portugal that the French had passed through, pillaging and destroying everything they found and raping every woman, old and young.

"What will happen to us?" Elvina asked aloud, looking out at St. Jean de Luz.

It looked so peaceful and quiet. Just a little French village. But she knew that Bayonne, only a few kilometres away up the coast, was one of the major bases of French troops.

She washed her hands and face, tidied the cabin a little and, making quite sure that there was no possibility of anyone looking at her through the keyhole or through a crack in the walls, she readjusted the dispatches in her bodice, making them at once more comfortable and more secure.

And then, because she knew that, even if she lay down, she would never sleep, she went back to the main cabin.

The French Officer was still drinking, but in other parts of the ship there was the sound of hammering and men moving about and of work being done.

"I wonder if my daughter might entertain you for a few minutes while I change my clothes?" Lord Wye asked. "They are wet and as you see, I am extremely dishevelled. I was just thinking of changing when you came aboard."

The Frenchman looked at him suspiciously.

"Are you trying to escape me?" he asked.

"It would be quite impossible, would it not?" Lord Wye smiled. "And I am leaving you my daughter as a hostage."

"Very well," the Frenchman said ungraciously.

"I will leave the door open if that is what you wish," Lord Wye suggested.

"No, no your daughter is here," the Commodore replied.

Elvina thought that he was being magnanimous, but as soon as the door was closed, he leaned forward across the table.

"Is that man really your father?" he asked in French.

Elvina, who spoke French as well as she spoke Portuguese, deliberately hesitated and then answered with an accent as noticeable as Lord Wye's,

"*Mais oui*! He is – my Papa. Did he not tell you so?"

"How old are you?"

"Thirteen years old – nearly fourteen," Elvina replied.

The Commodore seemed to believe this and sat back in his chair.

"You are wise to leave Lisbon," he said. "You ought to have brought your mother with you. Marshal Soult will drive the British into the sea and the Portuguese will be punished for harbouring them."

"Marshal Soult?" Elvina questioned, her eyebrows raised.

"Yes, he has arrived at Bayonne. The Emperor sent him and now soon there will be no more fighting in Spain."

Elvina had heard of the Marshal and knew that he was one of Napoleon's greatest Generals.

"The Emperor must be very angry – about the victory at Vitoria," she said timidly.

"Angry! Of course he is not angry. It was not really a victory. We have not enough troops in Spain at the moment. They have been engaged on the Russian front. Now that Marshal Soult is here, that little upstart Army will soon be in retreat."

The Commodore seemed so cocksure that Elvina felt her spirits drop.

"*Voilà*, but a little girl like you should not worry your head about war," he added. "You should find other things to occupy your mind."

He leered at her across the table and poured himself another glass of wine and Elvina was thankful when a few minutes later Lord Wye returned.

He had changed completely and he looked very resplendent in a coat as blue as the summer sea, white breeches, a high, snowy white cravat and boots polished until the whole cabin seemed reflected in them.

He wore a ring on his finger and a jewelled fob hung from his vest pocket. He might just have been going for a walk down St. James's Street or making a call on the Prince Regent at Carlton House.

The Frenchman gaped at him, forgetting to drink in his astonishment at such elegance.

Elvina sprang to her feet.

"Oh, you have taken off the bandage!" she exclaimed.

"I hoped you would tie me another one," Lord Wye answered with a smile. "I am afraid the wound is still bleeding a trifle."

"I must bathe it too," Elvina said. "It looks inflamed – I hope you do not have a splinter in it."

"You must forgive these little domestic details, *monsieur*," Lord Wye smiled. "My daughter fusses over me, I excuse her natural anxiety because her mother gave her such explicit instructions to look after me on the homeward voyage."

"You are a lucky man," the Commodore replied. *"Malheureusement*, I am unmarried and have no one to look after me."

"That is indeed a tragedy," Lord Wye commented.

He turned to Elvina.

"You will find clean bandages and a bowl which you can fill with water in my cabin, my dear."

"Oh, thank you –" Elvina replied. Then, feeling the Frenchman's eyes on her, she added a little awkwardly, " – Papa".

'There is some reason for his sending me into the cabin,' she thought as she went towards the door. Once she was inside she realised what it was.

There were indeed two bandages laid out on a table fixed against the wall, but when she picked them up she found underneath a purse heavy with money. She concealed the purse in the pocket of her petticoat.

Then she picked up the basin and saw a piece of paper and another purse.

"*If you get the chance*," she read, "*give this to the Captain.*"

The purse contained guineas, she thought, and hiding it in her hand beneath the basin, she went back into the cabin and laid the bandages down on the table.

"I must have clean water for your wound," she said. "Shall I go on deck and draw some from the water barrels?"

"I think that would be wisest," Lord Wye answered. "My head is throbbing and I am only hoping that it is not infected."

Without waiting for the Frenchman's permission Elvina went through the door onto the deck. In one quick glance she saw the Captain standing by the broken mast, giving orders to a seaman.

Two Frenchmen with cocked muskets were near him listening suspiciously it seemed to her to what he was saying, although it was doubtful if they could understand a word.

Elvina walked across to him.

"Oh, Captain. Lord Wye has asked me if you will fetch him some clean water from the water butts," she said and thrust the basin into his arms.

The Captain looked up in surprise and was just about to suggest that the seaman should take the basin when he felt Elvina's hand underneath it. He took the purse from her automatically and she left the basin with him saying,

"Please draw the water for me, I am not certain how to do it for myself."

Turning she smiled at the two French seamen to distract their attention from the Captain.

"It is a lovely day, *messieurs*, is it not?" she asked in French.

"Who taught you to speak our language?" one of them enquired.

"Your countrymen in the prison camps of Lisbon," Elvina replied. "I have often been there to visit them and I have written letters for those who were ill in hospital and unable to write home."

"*Eh bien!*" one of them answered. "Come here, *ma petite*, and give me a kiss."

He put out his hand towards her, but Elvina sidestepped adroitly.

"I have work to do. Your Commodore will be angry if I am away too long."

She ran down the deck after the Captain who had reached the water butt and was filling the basin. She knew by now that the purse would be safe within his pocket.

"Thank his Lordship," he said in a low voice.

She did not answer him, fearing that they might be overheard, but merely smiled, took the basin from him and went back to the cabin.

The Frenchman was still talking somewhat expansively now about the brilliant Generalship of Marshal Soult and the victories he had won on other fronts.

"How soon do you think he plans his attack?" Lord Wye asked.

The Frenchman shrugged his shoulders.

"Today, tomorrow, yesterday! Marshal Soult is always in a hurry. He does not let the grass grow under his feet. Before you can say '*allons-y*' he will be across the Pyrénées and then your long-nosed General Wellington will have to look out."

The day seemed to pass very slowly.

After luncheon, while the Frenchman drank more wine and talked still more boastfully, Lord Wye suggested that the bandages on his head should be changed again.

Under the basin Elvina found another package of money, this time a slightly bigger one, and on a piece of paper he had written,

"For Mister Sanders and tell him to distribute three guineas to each of our men on board."

She tore up the paper and also the first message that Lord Wye had written into tiny pieces and threw them out of the porthole. Then she took her basin on deck. Fortunately Mister Sanders was by the deckhouse and she passed the package to him as she had done to the Captain.

This time it was a little more difficult because she had to deliver the message and although she did not think that the Frenchmen who were near them could understand English, she did not dare take a chance.

"His Lordship says give the men as much water as they wish," she said at length indicating the water in the butt. "He suggests three pints for each."

Mister Sanders gave her a slight almost imperceptible wink and she knew that he understood.

"Tell his Lordship it'll be as he wishes," he answered.

The tide had turned and was coming in again. The breeze was freshening a little and the waves were slapping against the yacht.

At last the French Commodore began to stir himself. He ordered the French seamen to get the towrope ready and to manoeuvre their ship into position.

Lord Wye went on deck with him and offered all possible assistance.

It was then that Elvina realised he was deliberately playing for time. The towrope that had been provided and which had lain waiting all the afternoon proved to be too short.

Others were procured only to snap unaccountably as soon as any strain was put on them.

The French Commodore began shouting instructions and the men in the ship shouted back.

The Captain, peculiarly flustered it seemed to Elvina over a very small matter compared with what they had all been through last night, gave orders and countermanded them so that the men ran first in one direction, then in another and finally achieved nothing.

'What is Lord Wye waiting for?' she wondered.

She looked out to sea and knew that any hope of rescue by an English ship was quite out of the question. The English might have a free passage in the Bay, but they were not so foolish as to come so far inshore.

Besides what would be the point when the direct route from England lay off Cape Finisterre and down to Lisbon,

Again and again something went wrong with the towrope. Again and again the yacht seemed about to float, the Frenchmen strained at their oars and nothing happened.

Time passed. It was very hot, so hot that the Frenchmen, sweating and straining, began to curse and grow disagreeable.

There was a fierce altercation between the Commodore and his second-in-command. Both grew crimson in the face as they gesticulated and threw their arms about

"It is time for a rest," Lord Wye suggested cheerfully. "Let's splice the main brace for everyone. Come on, *monsieur*, join me in a tot of rum. It will do us all good."

The rum, and a very large ration of it, ladled out under a hot sun, made everyone seem to sweat the more. But still the yacht would not move.

It was past seven o'clock and the sun was sinking before finally they achieved a small movement in her position.

A cheer went up from the French ship.

This time the towrope was holding and slowly, very slowly she was coming to starboard.

"Row, *curse you!*" the Commodore shouted at them. "Row! *Row!*"

By straining every muscle and every sinew the Frenchmen got her off the sandbank and out to sea.

"They have done it! Congratulations, *monsieur,* a very fine piece of work!" Lord Wye exclaimed. "It was entirely due to your ideas and your organisation. I do indeed congratulate you."

Elvina could not help but be amused to see how the Frenchman lapped up the flattery.

"And now we must celebrate, *monsieur,*" Lord Wye went on. "You have done the impossible. You have saved my yacht. She is afloat and before we go onshore, another drink is obviously called for. There is no hurry now."

He raised his hands to his mouth,

"Splice the main brace!" he shouted.

The French seamen, who understood what this meant if they understood no other word of English, cheered heartily.

"No, no, we will go into Harbour right away," the Commodore expostulated.

"You could not be so unkind when they have worked so hard," Lord Wye said taking his arm. "Come back to the cabin and we will split a bottle of something really worth having."

He gave a signal to the Captain. Already another barrel of rum had been rolled up on deck and the Frenchmen had stopped rowing and were standing up shouting for it

"*Non*! *Non*! *Etes-vous fou*?" the Commodore began.

But he had drunk too much for too long and he was not used to the quality of the wine that Lord Wye had been plying him with.

There was brandy on the cabin table, brandy so strong that he hiccoughed after a few sips.

"Magnificent stuff!" Lord Wye said raising his glass as if to a toast.

"*Dites donc*, we must get on. We must get into the Harbour!" the Commodore cried.

At the same time he took a long drink of the cognac and then another.

Lord Wye filled his glass again.

"To your good fortune, *monsieur*, and may you find a beautiful woman to share it with."

The Frenchman rocked with laughter at that.

"I can find lots of women to share my fortune," he said. "Too many. What I want is a steady sensible wife with a big dowry."

"Ah! They are hard to come by," Lord Wye answered.

"*Il n'y a plus à dire!*" the Frenchman exclaimed. "But now Marshal Soult is arriving, we shall see some very beautiful women in Bayonne. *Voilà une idée*, my Lord, if you are imprisoned in Bayonne, you will be able to see them from the prison windows! It should amuse you, even though you cannot get any nearer."

He laughed again and Elvina felt a sudden fury shake her. How dare he mock them? How dare he talk in such a way? She felt hot words rising to her lips.

As if he knew what she was thinking, Lord Wye gave her a warning glance.

"You must come and visit me, *monsieur*, and then perhaps I shall be able to advise you on which one to choose."

The Commodore thought that this so funny that he almost fell off his chair. While he was laughing Lord Wye filled up his glass, but made no effort to replenish his own.

From outside came the sound of laughter and coarse jokes being shouted by the Frenchmen.

The Englishmen drank, but silently, sullenly resentful at being made prisoners, hating their captors but realising there was nothing they could do but to await incarceration in some stinking French prison, where they would remain, if they did not die, until the end of hostilities.

The time was passing and Lord Wye sent for another bottle of cognac. The Frenchman expostulated, but by now he was finding it a little difficult to say anything very articulately.

Outside on deck another barrel of rum was brought up from down below.

"*Avis*! We must go! We must go!"

The Frenchman swept the bottle off the table and rose to his feet.

"To the Harbour, *à toute vitesse*!" he shouted and the cry was taken up by his second-in-command.

"To the Harbour!"

The French seamen put out their oars again and Elvina, going onto the deck, noticed that some of them were a little unsteady, but the majority were tough and the drink had merely made them noisy.

"Slowly! Take her slowly!" Lord Wye said anxiously. "The tow-rope will break again."

His prophesy came true about a quarter of an hour later. The Captain had been inspecting the rope a few minutes earlier and then unaccountably it broke and the yacht was adrift while the men struggled to find a fresh rope.

What with the inefficiency of the English in not being able to connect the rope and dropping it several times into the sea, it was nearly an hour before they were in tow again.

By this time they seemed to have drifted some way down the coast so that it was an even longer journey to the Harbour of St. Jean de Luz.

They managed about a quarter of a mile and the same thing happened. This time the Commodore was in a frenzy.

"Get the ship into Harbour!" he ordered his men. "Arrange it yourselves. These damned English are putting a curse on it"

He turned angrily to Lord Wye.

"I believe your men are deliberately delaying matters," he shouted. "It will not do them any good. They are my prisoners and there is no chance of any escape."

"We are all convinced of that," Lord Wye replied quietly. "But if you prefer it, I will tell them to let your men do everything themselves."

He knew that the Commodore was short-handed and did not wish to spare a man to take over the wheel of the yacht.

"*Non! Non! Continuez,*" the Frenchman muttered. "*Nous avons besoin de tous.*"

"One thing, the steering is quite all right," Lord Wye said comfortably.

He walked cross the deck as if to reassure himself. Elvina, watching him, saw him say something to the Captain and stroll back again towards the Commodore.

What did he plan? Was there any chance of escape?

There were only eight Englishmen whole and unwounded against thirty Frenchmen.

It was impossible, she thought. And besides the Frenchmen all had muskets. She could see the firing pieces lying beside them and the man at the tiller of the French ship had one in his left hand.

Anxiously she looked out to sea. Not a sign of an English ship.

The Frenchmen had now fixed the rope.

"Keep away from it!" the Commodore cried to an English sailor. "Keep away, all of you!"

He drew a pistol from his belt.

"I will shoot the first man who goes near it. This time I will watch it myself."

He glared round the deck at the Englishmen and turned to shout to his own men,

"Start rowing. Take it slowly! Don't hurry. We will get this yacht into Harbour or I will clap the whole lot of you in irons!"

It was a drunken threat, but Elvina could see that the French seamen were impressed. It was the sort of language they understood.

The yacht was moving. Slowly and inexorably they were being towed towards St. Jean de Luz. Elvina looked towards the Harbour. For the first time she realised that the sun was sinking.

It was a shining glory in the West, going down, golden and scarlet, over the sea, while above the first stars had appeared, twinkling where the sky changed from pale lucent gold to the first sable fingers of night.

"May my daughter and I pack a few personal items, *monsieur*?" Lord Wye asked the Commodore respectfully.

"You can pack them," was the answer, "But I'll be guillotined before I let you take anything valuable ashore. When I get you into Harbour, we will soon see to that."

Elvina saw Lord Wye's eyes flicker, but he merely smiled.

"Come along, my dear," he said to Elvina.

He drew her into the cabin, closed the door quietly and then bolted it.

"Quick!" he said. "We have no time to lose."

"What are – we going to do?"

Lord Wye went across the cabin to the porthole. He pulled it open. It was more ornamental than any of the others on the yacht with the glass set in small leaded panes. When it was open, it was large enough to admit the body of a man.

Elvina watched him wide-eyed.

"You can swim, I suppose?" he asked almost as an afterthought.

"I have swum all my life."

"Good. You see that beach to the North of the Harbour. We will make for that. If they shoot at us and hit me, go on. Don't wait for anyone.

"I have told the Captain that every man is to fend for himself as soon as they get inside the Harbour. If anything happens to me, try and find one of the others or make your own way home. Is that understood?"

She nodded.

Somehow it was impossible to speak at such a moment.

"I am sorry, my child," he said gently. "It would have been safer for you to have remained at Lisbon."

"I am not sorry I came," Elvina replied. "Even if I die now – it has been worth it."

He smiled at that and then lifted her up in his arms. Just for a moment he held her close as if to comfort her. Then he pushed her through the porthole.

She clung for a moment to his hands, looking down at the water beneath her, before she dropped.

She felt the sudden chill, felt the waves close over her head and then she was striking out, swimming for the shore with strong strokes, conscious only of the encumbrance of her skirts around her legs and that her slippers had already left her feet.

Behind her she heard another splash and knew that Lord Wye was in the water. There was no time to look back.

She knew that every foot they put between themselves and the yacht meant a greater degree of safety.

How soon would they be missed? How soon would someone realise what was happening?

They must have gone nearly fifty yards before she heard a shout. One of the men in the boat had spotted them and was pointing them out to the Commodore.

There was more shouting and then Elvina looked over her shoulder.

Someone ran across the deck and began hammering on the cabin door. They were still not sure it was them.

"Don't look back," she heard Lord Wye say beside her. "Hurry! Keep swimming."

She obeyed him and now the voices seemed to be growing a little fainter. There was a sudden report of a shot. Now she could not help but look back again and saw that a shot had been fired into the air.

The Commodore had taken aim at them, but the Captain had struck his arm upwards and the shot had exploded harmlessly.

She could hear his shout of fury and distinctly across the water came the command to shoot.

The men in the boat were levelling their muskets, but what with the drink, the movement of the sea and the fact that she and Lord Wye were nearly out of range, they could hear the reports, but the bullets were nowhere near them.

"Hurry! Hurry!" Lord Wye was saying.

She felt her soaked gown dragging her legs and wondered how Lord Wye was managing in his boots.

Then she saw that he had taken off his coat and was swimming without it. His boots had gone too. She had a sudden glimpse of a white-stockinged foot.

"Come on!" he called. "We have to hurry!"

There were more shots, but now they were far away.

Elvina suddenly felt the shingle scrape her knees and she scrambled to her feet.

The beach was mercifully deserted. It was to the North of the town and beyond it there were no houses, only some fir trees growing on the edge of the sand.

"Hurry!" Lord Wye said again.

He dragged her by the arm and she struggled to keep up with him. The stones were hurting her feet.

She wished she could stop and wring out the skirt of her gown, but she dared not suggest it.

They were running now over the sand and into the shadow of the trees. Elvina was gasping for breath when finally Lord Wye let go of her arm and turned to stare back the way they had come.

Far in the distance in the dusk he could see the boat towing the yacht. It was not yet in Harbour and the men did not seem to be rowing very well.

There was certainly nothing rhythmical about it.

"We are safe!" Elvina gasped.

Lord Wye looked about him.

"Not safe," he answered. "We have only exchanged one difficult situation for another."

CHAPTER FIVE

"I think we have about half an hour before they begin to look for us," Lord Wye said quietly. "By this time some of my men will have escaped as well, so we may be certain that they will send out quite a large force."

"What can we do?" Elvina asked, looking at him.

Even with his clothes wet and clinging to his figure it was impossible not to realise that anyone seeing him would recognise him for what he was, a gentleman of fashion.

"We had better start moving," Lord Wye suggested.

But she heard the note of despair in his voice and realised that already he felt that there was little chance of their not being recaptured.

They trudged through the trees, Elvina lifting her wet skirts high in her hands to prevent them from clinging round her legs and impeding her progress.

Once she stumbled and Lord Wye put out his hand and took her arm, helping her along.

'We must escape. We must get away,' she told herself.

She felt that they were like a hunted hare who must run in a circle and find danger on every side.

South of them, as Elvina well knew, lay the Pyrénées, held by Napoleon's troops. To the North of them was Bayonne with Marshal Soult gathering a large Army together, ready for a fresh attack on the Duke of Wellington. Behind them was the sea.

'There must be somewhere we can go – *somewhere*,' Elvina told herself.

She started to pray with an intensity that seemed to her to strain her whole body, mind and soul with the urgency of her plea.

'Please, God, let us find a way, *please*.'

She must have closed her eyes, because she felt Lord Wye stop abruptly, his hand tightening on her arm. She looked and saw what had stopped him!

In front of them was a camp of soldiers. There were a few tents, but most of them were bivouacking in the open.

They were sitting round fires, there were women preparing meals, there were children playing around the baggage carts and there was the usual indefinable paraphernalia which are part and parcel of every camp, stretching away, it seemed to Elvina, indefinitely into the distance.

Quickly Lord Wye pulled her back into the shadow of some thick bushes.

"Troops!" he whispered. "We cannot walk through them."

Despairing Elvina looked towards the town. What could they do now? To go back was hopeless, to go forward was impossible.

Suddenly she gave a little exclamation.

About one hundred and fifty yards away from them there were some large tents and outside them a pitiful queue of soldiers waiting patiently in the dusk.

Elvina had seen this scene so often, seen the men on crutches or supported by their comrades, seen their roughly-bandaged heads and arms and the blood staunched usually with nothing more than a dirty rag waiting miserably but without complaint for medical attention.

She drew a quick breath.

"Listen," she breathed to Lord Wye. "I have thought of – something. You see that hospital tent – over there?"

Lord Wye nodded.

"When men die," she told him, "they throw out their uniforms and there is generally a pile of them waiting for collection. They take them to the quartermaster's stores and issue them again."

"A pile of them?" Lord Wye questioned.

He understood without a waste of words what she was trying to convey to him and his eyes lit with a sudden hope.

"I will go and look," Elvina said, "You stay here."

"No, no, of course you cannot," Lord Wye expostulated. "I will go."

If it had not been so dangerous Elvina would have laughed.

"How far do you think you would get?" she asked. "No one will notice me. Look at the women over there – the children playing in the dust. I am not much different from any of them, you can see that. Keep hidden. Stay here. If it is impossible for me to take anything – I will come back at once."

"You swear that?" Lord Wye asked.

He put his hands on her shoulders and turned her round to face him.

Then he tipped her face up to his.

"Listen, child," he said softly. "There is no need for you to stay with me. Go now and hide yourself in the town. You speak French and there are, I am certain, a hundred dialects gathered in St. Jean de Luz. No one will suspect that you are Portuguese. Say you are French from a different Province. Someone will take compassion on you, some honest burgher or his wife. Go now while you are still free. You have little chance with me."

"Do you think I want to take the hospitality – or even ask a kindness of the enemy?" Elvina asked. "I would rather die."

In Lord Wye's eyes she saw a little flicker of admiration or pleasure and she added,

"I will stay with you whatever happens. You have been very kind to me. Perhaps in some way I can repay that debt."

He released his hold on her and with a smile said,

"There is no debt."

"Then we can share the danger – together."

He took her hand in his –

"Your courage makes me ashamed."

"We must not stay here talking," Elvina said with a sudden urgency. "Wait here. Don't be seen. I will be as quick – as I can."

"For God's sake be careful," Lord Wye begged of her.

"Don't worry," she replied.

She slipped away through the trees.

As she neared the hospital tent, she was in sight both of the camp and of the men waiting outside it, but, as she had suspected, no one paid the slightest attention to her,

Her clothes were dried a little by this time. They were damp, but the dampness made little difference to the faded cotton, now stained by the seawater.

The men waiting outside the hospital tent did not even pay her the compliment of a second glance. They were waiting with sullen faces and Elvina, who had heard how the French met defeat, guessed that some of them were from Vitoria.

Through the open flaps of the tent she could see that the place was crowded. There was another tent beyond it and yet another. At all of them were the same queues of wounded and occasionally there was a cry of agony or a man shouting in a delirium of fever.

The orderlies, rough and often drunken, were flinging the slops and the blood onto the sandy ground outside the tents and, sure enough, as Elvina had expected, there were other things piled up outside.

Corpses awaiting burial were inadequately shrouded with old blankets and sometimes the same one served two bodies. The dead men's feet, protruding from the inadequate covering, were bare and Elvina knew they had already been stripped.

Slowly she moved between the tents. No one noticed her, everyone was too busy to wonder what the dark-haired dirty-looking child could be doing.

She found what she was seeking, a large pile of French uniforms, and even as she came upon it another tunic came whizzing through the side of the tent to fall on the pile and was followed by a pair of trousers.

Most of the uniforms were in a deplorable state. The mud and the rain had soaked into them until the original colouring was almost lost.

Buttons were missing, what should have been blue was now a dirty grey and there were great rents in the sleeves, while many of the seats to the trousers were worn completely away.

Elvina started delving amongst the pile. She was not shocked or even disgusted by what she saw and had to do. She was intent only on one thing – saving the life of the man who had rescued her.

Whatever Lord Wye might know about French prisons, she knew what those in Lisbon were like.

She had seen the conditions that the prisoners lived under, often starved and ill-treated by their warders and without medical attention for their wounds so that death would be at times a merciful release.

'This might do,' she murmured beneath her breath.

She found what she was seeking, a tunic that looked bigger than most of the others. It was worn and faded but not particularly ragged and, turning over the dirty garments, she found a pair of breeches that were also in a reasonable condition.

She had no illusions as to what would happen to her if she was caught stealing. Fortunately everyone was too busy inside the tents to wonder what was occurring outside.

Boots were her next problem. She guessed that Lord Wye would have a large foot. But the boots were in a deplorable condition, the soles almost worn away, the uppers cracked and the laces non-existent.

There was not much time to choose. Elvina's instinct told her that already she had been searching too long.

She took the largest pair of boots she could find and placing all she had collected in her skirt, lifted it as the peasant women did when they collected sticks for their fires.

She was only just in time. An orderly, coming from the tent to throw yet another dead man's clothes onto the pile, saw her moving away.

"Hey!" he shouted. "What are you doing? Get away from here or it'll be the worse for you."

Burdened as she was, Elvina managed to run. For a moment she thought that he might come after her, but it was obviously too much trouble.

He shouted something rude but unintelligible and went back into the tent.

Moving down amongst the trees out of sight of the camp, Elvina found her way back to Lord Wye. For a moment, when she reached the clump of shrubs where she had left him, she could not see him and her heart gave a sudden frightened leap of sheer fear.

Then he called her name softly.

"Elvina, I am here!"

She made her way to him through the bushes and found that he had hidden himself in the hole made by a tree that had fallen in the winter gales.

"Have you found anything?"

Standing above him, she looked down and then slowly let the skirt of her gown drop so that the trousers, tunic and boots fell at his feet.

"Clever child!"

His voice was warm with approval.

"Hurry and change," she urged. "Don't waste time. I have a feeling that they may appear at any moment."

She turned her back and went to watch the camp through the bushes. Many of the soldiers had settled themselves down for the night.

Their tunics were off and they used them as pillows, turning their faces away from the fires and seeking the shelter of a wagon or a pile of baggage.

Others were laughing or flirting with the women, one or two were frankly making love, quite oblivious of those around them.

"These boots are damned tight!" Elvina heard Lord Wye exclaim.

She turned back to him and for the moment she could not help laughing. He looked so comical pulling at his boots, white hands stretching out of the shabby tunic.

They were obviously too tight.

"The only thing to do," Lord Wye said, "is for me to release the front of these boots. They are already bursting from the seams and really I should be more comfortable with nothing at all on my feet."

"Let your toes burst out of them," Elvina agreed. "Many men over there are wearing boots in a far worse state. Remember you are supposed to have walked back here from Vitoria. It is quite a long way."

"About sixty miles I imagine," Lord Wye replied, "and over mountainous country. Poor devils! I would sympathise with them if I did not know that our own men will be advancing over it shortly."

"Now? At this moment?" Elvina asked.

Her eyes met Lord Wye's and they both thought the same thing at the same time.

"That is what we will do," he said softly. "We will join up with Wellington's Army."

"How can we without being discovered?"

"Marshal Soult will be going into action almost at once if the Commodore is to be believed. You have seen an Army on the march, the baggage carts, the women, the hangers-on, those who have been wounded, but who wish to regain their Regiments, trail along behind. That is where we will be, Elvina, behind Marshal Soult's Army and when Wellington breaks through we will be there to welcome him."

"And supposing he doesn't?" Elvina asked.

"He will," Lord Wye answered confidently. "And what is the alternative? To walk through France? It is a long way to the English Channel and we would be in enemy country all the time."

"No, you are right," Elvina said. "It is our – only hope. But supposing they discover us?"

Lord Wye shrugged his shoulders.

"Don't let us anticipate anything so unpleasant," he said. "They must not discover us."

"You speak French," Elvina said reflectively, "but with such an accent."

"Dammit! I have had the best teachers. I always rather fancied myself!"

Elvina laughed.

"It might be all right for exchanging Diplomatic pleasantries," she said, "but a Frenchman would know at once that you were not one of his countrymen."

She gave a little cry.

"I have it! Listen to me."

Lord Wye looked over his shoulder.

"Speak lower. We don't want to be overheard."

As he spoke, he picked up his discarded garments and thrust them deep into a rabbit hole at the foot of a tree.

"Now," he said. "What is your idea?"

"You have been – wounded," Elvina said, looking at the bandage round his head. "You were hit in the head by a British bullet and although you wish to get back into the firing line, you are still dazed and perhaps – a little mental from what you have been through. I am looking after you, so I will speak for you. I will explain that you have been very brave, but are just a trifle mad."

"Mad!" Lord Wye exclaimed. "I don't think that is a part I particularly want to play."

"It is safe. Do you not see how safe it is?" Elvina said. "All you have to do is to walk along looking rather stupid. And now, while I think of it – do something to your face, to your hands and to your fingernails. Do you suppose that any French soldier who has been into battle looks as clean as that? Besides – you are so fair."

"I have already thought of that while you were away," Lord Wye answered. "If anyone asks we must say I am from Brittany. The Frenchmen who come from there are very like the English, tall, often blue-eyed and fair-skinned."

"Even so you would still have been out working in the fields or on the sea. Fortunately you are sunburned, but you still look too clean and your hands are too white."

She looked around. There were some berries growing on one of the shrubs. She tried one on her own hands and realised that it had juice that was dark in appearance.

She picked a handful and going to Lord Wye, who was busy pushing his fingers into the earth round the uprooted tree to get his nails dirty, took his hand in hers and started to rub them into his skin.

She felt the strength of his fingers despite their fine bones. She wondered that they could be both strong and gentle.

"That is a good idea of yours," Lord Wye said approvingly and then suddenly he bent and kissed her cheek. "I have not thanked you yet, child, for all you have done for me. If it was not for you, I should already be languishing in irons."

She felt his lips burn against her skin. She bent her head to prevent him from seeing the sudden wave of scarlet that had crept up her cheeks.

He kissed her as he might have kissed any child, and yet, because in reality she was a woman, she could not accept it in the same light-hearted way that it had been given.

Her first kiss! She felt in some extraordinary way that it was a monumental moment and yet in fact she had no time to think about it.

"Your hands are – better," she said abruptly, "and now I must do – your shirt."

"No one will see it underneath the tunic," he said.

"You might open it by mistake," she answered. "Over there the men are in their shirtsleeves. If you did the same, your shirt would attract immediate attention."

He had thrown away his cravat, but the whiteness and the fineness of his linen made it quite unsuitable for an ordinary soldier.

Obediently Lord Wye took off his tunic and for a moment Elvina hesitated. She knew that in reality he ought to discard his shirt altogether, but she could not bring herself to ask him to do so.

She knew how much he would hate to have the dirt and sweat of another man's rough uniform coat against his skin, and so she set to work with berries and the soil around them to make the shirt look as dirty and dilapidated as possible.

His chest was hard beneath the softness of his shirt and she felt her fingers quiver because she was touching him and it was difficult to remember the danger and the urgency.

She could only think that he was a man and she was trembling for some reason that she could not understand.

"And now what do we do?" Lord Wye asked.

He was disguised, there was no doubt about that. With the bandage round his head he looked as she had seen so many wounded men look, dishevelled and rather unkempt.

"We dare not stay here," Elvina cautioned. "If they search the woods, they are certain to think it strange that we have hidden ourselves away. Come, we must be brave and sit near the hospital tents as if you had just had your head attended to."

Walking slowly because his boots hurt him, Lord Wye struggled through the bushes and out into the wood.

"Now slouch a little, don't walk so erect," Elvina admonished him. "And look stupid, as if you were still half-unconscious from the bullet wound."

They moved through the wood as far as the tents and then, with Elvina holding her breath in fear, they stepped out into the open. There was still a long queue waiting outside the hospital tents.

They sank down at the foot of one of the trees not very far from it. They were in the shadows, the flies buzzed round them and the noise of the camp seemed to encompass them.

They were only just in time. They had not been there for more than two or three minutes when from the woods behind them came the sound of voices, of men calling to each other as they beat their way through the bushes and trampled down the undergrowth.

"Cover your head," Lord Wye said suddenly in a hoarse whisper. "They might recognise you."

Elvina pulled up her gown and deliberately tore a strip from the hem of her cotton petticoat. The sand had stuck to it when it was wet and many washes had already yellowed and discoloured it. She tied it peasant-fashion over her head and under her chin.

"Now, don't forget," she said almost beneath her breath, "whatever they say to you, take no notice. You do not understand. You do not even hear – "

The men were coming nearer. She did not dare to turn her head to look at them. It was best to seem unconcerned. She glanced at Lord Wye as he deliberately shrunk his head on his shoulders as if he was asleep.

His legs, with his toes sticking through the broken boots, were out in front of him. No one would suspect, she thought, that only a few hours ago he had appeared in the cabin of his own yacht looking the very picture of elegance.

The men who were searching the wood had reached them and came through the trees and into the camp. They were none of them the men who had been in the boat, Elvina thought.

They were seamen whom the Commodore must have ordered out from their Barracks to hunt for the fugitives.

"Comrade, have you seen an Englishman accompanied by a child?" she heard one of them ask the wounded waiting outside the hospital tents.

"If there was an Englishman here, you wouldn't see him alive," the man answered. "*Mère de Dieu*, but may the whole race rot like our corpses on those accursed mountains."

The seaman gave no answer to this and walked away to join his compatriots. They talked among themselves and then moved through the camp asking questions here and there, but in a very perfunctory manner.

They were obviously quite assured that Lord Wye would not have dared to appear where there were soldiers.

Now that they were gone Elvina was conscious of the tension she had suffered. Without knowing it she had dug her nails into the palm of her hand and her lip was bleeding a little because her teeth had caught her lip to stop it trembling.

Lord Wye must suddenly have become aware of her agitation for he reached out and took her hand in his.

"They have gone," he said quietly, "and we are still free."

She turned to him with a little sob.

"I was afraid," she whispered. "I would never have believed – that I could be so afraid. I thought at any moment they would discover you."

"We are cleverer than they are," he answered. "You must believe that. Confidence is the one thing that will carry us through any situation, however desperate."

But now the danger was past and Elvina was still trembling. She put her free hand to her breast as if to still the tumult there and was suddenly conscious of the Duke of Wellington's dispatches.

She made a little sound that was half a cry and half a laugh. Lord Wye's fingers on hers were very warm and strong.

"It's a desperate adventure," he said gently. "But we are going to win through, you and I. Do you hear me, Elvina? Stop trembling and listen to me. We are going to win through. We are going to reach the British Army. I know it in my bones."

She laughed a little tremulously at the expression.

"That is better," he smiled. "You have been so brave up till now. In fact, if it was not for you, we should not be here. Now there are more obstacles ahead, but I am utterly convinced that we shall surmount them all."

She felt as if his words, the look in his eyes and the touch of his hand hypnotised her.

She began to believe it was possible that they would succeed. Their whole plan was wild, mad and crazy, she thought, an adventure that only two people who were really a little deranged in the head would undertake.

And yet, because there was no alternative, they would attempt it.

"Do you trust me, Elvina?" she heard Lord Wye ask.

She looked up at him, her lips still quivering a little, but her eyes were as clear and trusting as those of a child.

"Yes," she said. "I too have a feeling that we shall reach the Duke of Wellington."

It was all very well to have faith in their ultimate goal, but they were both hungry and thirsty. The hospital tents were closing and the men waiting were dispersing. Soon it would be fully dark.

"We must have food," Elvina said. "The troops will already have received their rations for today."

"We can buy some," Lord Wye replied.

"What with?" she enquired.

He made a little grimace.

"English gold."

"It's too dangerous," she answered and then she gave an exclamation. "No, I have thought of a plan. Give me a guinea."

He delved into the pockets of his tunic and brought out a gold guinea. She held it in her hand. What she was going to do was a risk and yet, as they had taken so many risks, one more did not seem to matter.

She rose to her feet and walked towards the soldiers, choosing with care not the first but the second group, who looked to her older and more responsible than some of the others.

She went up to a Sergeant.

"*Pardon, Monsieur,*" she said, "but will you tell me where I can sell a pretty gold piece?"

"Gold piece?" the Sergeant asked. "And where would a child like you be getting' a gold piece?"

"From the man sitting over there by the hospital," she answered. "He took it from an English soldier on the battlefield. Now we are hungry and we want to eat. He has not been paid, although the Emperor owes him for nigh on six months."

This was drawing a bow at random. Elvina had heard how dilatory Napoleon was in paying his troops and anyway it was a condition that all Armies suffered from and all soldiers complained about it.

"Six months!" another soldier listening exclaimed. "Then he's lucky. I haven't been paid for two years."

"Let's look at your gold, child," the Sergeant said.

Elvina opened her hand and showed him the guinea lying on it. Then, before he could take it from her, closed her fingers again.

The Sergeant looked over his shoulder calculatingly at Lord Wye and Elvina guessed that he was wondering whether he dare take the money by force and keep it for himself or whether such action would cause trouble.

"I will give you thirty francs for it," he said at length.

It was robbery and Elvina knew it, but she did not dare protest.

"I will give you thirty-one," the other soldier piped up.

"Thirty is what I said," the Sergeant snapped at him. "It's not too bad for the pickings from a battlefield."

"*Merci, monsieur*," Elvina murmured. "We are hungry and my man is in no condition to fight his way to the food wagons."

"He'd be lucky if he got anythin' if he did," someone else exclaimed, while another soldier said mockingly,

"*Your* man! Can't he find anythin' bigger and more cuddlesome than a little skeleton like yourself?"

"I look after him all right," Elvina replied.

There was a laugh at this, but it was good-humoured. The Sergeant handed over the thirty francs. Elvina gave him the gold guinea and with a muttered, "*Merci bien, monsieur*," ran back to Lord Wye.

"He gave me thirty francs for it," she whispered.

"The thieving devil," Lord Wye replied.

"It does not matter. It will get us all we need. Get up now and we will go down to the town. Lean on my shoulder and keep your head down. You must not look tall or in good health for that matter."

They moved slowly away from the camp. It was not far to the town and, as Elvina expected, there was a market in the *Grande Place*.

There was not much to buy for the peasants had been plundered of almost all they possessed and therefore kept everything they could conceal from the ravishing thieving troops.

Elvina managed to buy some flour and, at an exorbitant price, half a dozen eggs, a tiny piece of cheese and some stale bread.

"Where can we eat?" she asked, looking round at the seething mob of people in the *Grande Place*.

"What about trying that Church?" Lord Wye suggested, pointing to the open door of an ancient building surmounted by a spire.

"But, of course," Elvina answered.

They slipped inside. Here there was emptiness, peace, the flicker of candles and the fragrance of incense.

Elvina dropped on her knees and said a prayer. Lord Wye did not kneel, but she felt that he too was praying for help.

They ate the bread and cheese, unable to wait any longer to satisfy their hunger.

"If we could find a fire, I would cook the eggs," Elvina said tentatively, still feeling hungry and knowing that Lord Wye's need must be greater than hers.

"Let's walk around for a little," he suggested. "No one will notice us in the crowd. I want to learn when the troops will be leaving."

It was dark when they came from the Church and went back to the *Grande Place*.

It seemed to be even more crowded than when they left it and from what was being said around them Elvina learnt that new troops had just arrived from the North. Many of them were only boys of sixteen, the Emperor's last batch of conscripts.

They looked worn out from a long march and many of them were obviously in ill health. At this moment they were all concerned with just one thing, getting something to eat.

Some were foraging about, trying to extort food from the people in the town, others were already cooking a meal over the fires they had lit in the streets and all along the quayside.

There were some women with them, some of them the ordinary hangers-on of the Army, blousy, cheap women who were prepared to sell their affections to whoever could pay for them. Others were wives and even mothers who had accompanied their menfolk into danger rather than to be left behind.

Choosing a motherly-looking woman who was cooking something that smelt delicious over a wood fire, Elvina approached her timidly.

"I have a few eggs, *madame*," she said. "Might we share your fire?"

The woman looked up, a refusal already on her lips and then she saw the bandage round Lord Wye's head.

"*Le pauvre brave!* He is wounded." she exclaimed.

Elvina nodded.

"Badly, *madame*. He cannot speak very well, but he can understand and he wishes to go back to fight again and this time to win."

"*Quel courage!*" the woman cried. "Sit down, *ma petite*. What have you with you? You can share some of our food as well, but we cannot give you much."

"I have only six eggs, *madame*. It was all I could buy."

"It's enough," the woman answered.

She cooked the eggs, making a rough omelette with goats' butter and herbs. Elvina shared some of it with her and her son and in return they gave both her and Lord Wye a piece of heavy dark bread such as the peasants bake.

Elvina felt that she had never eaten a more delicious meal and she knew, although he said nothing, that Lord Wye was enjoying it too.

"And now, *madame*, we must find somewhere to sleep," Elvina said. "Does your son know at what time the Army leaves tomorrow morning?"

The boy soldier, who had said little because he was too tired, roused himself to reply.

"Our orders are to stand by at dawn."

"You won't be well enough to go," his mother protested fiercely.

"As long as I can stand on two feet, they will make me," he answered sullenly.

"*Nom de Dieu!* When will this fiendish War end?" the woman asked despairingly. "First my husband and then my two elder sons have been taken from me. All I have left is Pierre and he has only just passed his sixteenth birthday."

"Oh, I am sorry," Elvina sympathised.

"What do we gain by war?" the woman asked. "*A quoi bon?* Our lands are laid waste, our fields are unploughed and our men are dead. What glory is there in that?"

"*Silence Mère*, that is traitorous talk," the boy urged.

"I know, I know," his mother went on. "But sometimes my heart feels that it will burst with keepin' back all one is afraid to say."

"We shall drive the English out," the boy said quickly. "That is why the Emperor has sent Marshal Soult to the front. He is a fine General."

"I only pray that you will be alive to see it," his mother moaned.

Elvina touched Lord Wye on the arm.

"*Allons-y*," she said.

She thanked the woman for her hospitality and then they started to find their way back towards the Church. A crowd of soldiers who had found their way into a wine cellar came reeling down the street and they were shouting,

"*Ou sont les femmes?* Bring out your women or we will come and get them!"

With a swift movement that Elvina had not expected, Lord Wye pushed her into a doorway of a house and stood in front of her.

"Keep quiet," he ordered. "These men are more dangerous than anything we have encountered so far."

Some of them burst into a shop that was still open and seized a girl from behind the counter. They dragged her into the street. Her shrieks echoed across the *Grande Place*, but no one made the slightest attempt to go to her rescue.

Drunken soldiers fought amongst themselves for her and then while she was still screaming one of them carried her away towards the beach.

"*Les femmes, les femmes! Nous desirous les femmes!*" the others yelled.

They reeled past the doorway where Lord Wye, looking suddenly somewhat aggressive, faced them.

Elvina felt the terror and horror of what was happening turn her knees to water. It was ghastly to wait behind Lord Wye and not run in search of safety.

It would have been a mad thing to do, but the waiting was almost too frightening to be endured.

Now the soldiers were level with them. She felt Lord Wye stiffen and knew that he would fight for her, but, strong and brave though he might be, he would have no chance against twenty or more men crazed with wine and lust.

She held onto his tunic in desperation and was almost flattened as Lord Wye's body pushed her back against the door until the carving on the wood bit into her skin.

"Are you wounded, soldier?" one of the men shouted. "Come and join us. A woman is better medicine than anything the doctor can give you."

There was a roar of laughter at this sally and they passed on, staggering and shouting, and before the noise had died away, the shrieks of another woman told Elvina that they had found a victim.

"Let's hurry," Lord Wye said grimly. "This is no place for you."

Forgetting all caution they ran down the side street that led to the Church. But here there was disappointment.

While they were gone, the Church had been closed and the door locked.

Elvina suggested that they should find a place to sleep in the graveyard.

"Even the drunken soldiers will seldom – go there," she muttered. "They are afraid of – ghosts."

"And are you not afraid of them?" Lord Wye asked.

"Not if you are with me," she answered simply.

They found a spot by a family vault. There was grass to sit on and the stone edifice to lean against.

It was quiet and the stars above them were gently reassuring.

Elvina gave a little sigh. It was one of relief, but Lord Wye misinterpreted it.

"Come and sit close to me, child. I will protect you somehow. And I swear to you I will kill the first man who puts his hands on you."

Elvina felt him draw her close and she let her head fall back against his chest.

"I am not afraid – with you," she whispered and knew that it was the truth.

CHAPTER SIX

The long winding column of men and mules climbed slowly up the rough mountain track towards the frontier.

Behind the file of soldiers in their stained and dusty uniforms, the sun glinting on their muskets, were the guns, pulled joltingly over the uneven going by bullock teams and followed by hundreds of peasants carrying shot and shell.

The bells on the mules mingled with the shouts of the muleteers and the screeching of wagons.

In contrast to the Commissionaires with their epaulettes and medals and the muleteers with their colourful rags and guitars, were the women who brought up the rear of the army.

The Officers' ladies, befeathered and bejewelled as no respectable wives would have been, were in carriages, while the women of the ordinary rank and file, looking tired and often heavy with child, trudged through the dust, but still had a ready tongue and a coarse joke for every man who spared them a glance.

Amongst these women marched the stragglers of the Army, the men who fell out from their columns during the march or who, incapacitated in some way or another, were determined not to be left behind.

Elvina noticed that there were several dozen in the same condition as Lord Wye, their heads bandaged or their arms in slings, but who still kept going.

They were often helped by some kindly women who would carry their muskets and even occasionally offered them a ride on a donkey, which were the possession of the more affluent.

"*Dites-moi, ma petite,* what's wrong with him?" a woman, whose painted face proclaimed her trade, asked Elvina, jerking her thumb in the direction of Lord Wye. "He hasn't said a word since we left the town."

"He is dazed and a little stupid from his wound," Elvina answered.

"Curses on the English who make us suffer in this way," the woman replied. "*Voilà, mon enfant,* you hang on to my donkey's tail. He won't kick you and it will give you a bit of help up the road."

Elvina thanked her and did as she suggested. Although Lord Wye was finding no difficulty in moving at the slow pace of the baggage column, she found that the rough stones hurt her feet and already one was cut and bleeding.

They had had quite an argument about shoes before they left.

"You must have shoes. You cannot walk with bare feet," Lord Wye had said. "We will knock up a shoemaker and buy a pair."

"And pay him with English gold, I suppose?" Elvina enquired. "Are you – crazy? It will make him suspicious. Besides a new pair of shoes will look ostentatious amongst the women I have seen behind the Armies – that is the respectable ones. They nearly all go bare-footed. It's only the Officers' women who can afford shoes."

"Dammit all!" Lord Wye expostulated.

"Don't worry," Elvina said quickly before he could argue any further. "I shall manage. My feet will get hardened – as do other women's."

"Other children's you mean," he said with a laugh. "I expect, if the truth were known, you like feeling free and untrammelled. I remember when I was a boy, walking through the fields in the early morning. I can still feel the cold of the dew on my bare feet. It is something I shall never forget."

Now Elvina rather regretted her impulse to be hard.

It was true that most of the other women who were, as she said, respectable, walked barefooted, but that was because the soldiers' pay was long overdue and when they did receive any money they spent it on clothes to cover their nakedness.

Their feet were as hard as leather and almost as dark as the army boots.

Lord Wye had been fortunate with his boots. When the muskets were distributed to the soldiers who had lost theirs, before they moved off in the morning, a contemptuous quartermaster who had doled out a musket and a pack had also chucked a pair of boots and gaiters at his feet.

"You're a disgrace to the Emperor!" he said sourly.

The boots were not new, but at least they were less worn and of a larger size than he was wearing already. The gaiters had lost several buttons, but they certainly smartened up his appearance.

"It is obvious," Lord Wye whispered to Elvina, "that Soult is having to scratch around to get an Army together. If they were not short of men they would not waste a musket on me."

The conversations that Elvina overheard confirmed this. Some of the Regiments that had straggled back from Vitoria and other battles in Spain were mere fragments mustering no more than two or three hundred men with the colours.

"He is certainly taking them young enough," Lord Wye exclaimed as he saw the thin emaciated boys, who had come from Northern France, marching past.

They were followed by veterans so tired and so worn by the exertions of war that they looked as if they might drop on their tracks even before they started.

But Marshal Soult himself was a legend and there was no doubt at all that the spirit of the new Army he had assembled to face Wellington with was inspired by their faith in him.

As the Officers passed them, a glittering cavalcade of good horseflesh, flying plumes and jingling decorations, Lord Wye nudged Elvina.

"That is Soult," he muttered.

She looked at the Marshal and felt a little shudder of fear. Aged forty-four, the same age as the Duke of Wellington, he was a big, rough coarse man.

There was a brutal look about him and she heard one of the women say later that he could be very vindictive if he did not get his own way or his troops did not do what he expected of them.

But it was not fear but admiration and the hope that he would lead them to victory that made the troops cheer as he rode amongst them, his shrewd hard eyes taking in every detail of the men he had to command.

"Now we will drive the devils into the sea!" a soldier shouted.

The Marshal heard him and replied,

"They must not be allowed to run. Kill them where they stand!"

There was a roar at this and Elvina felt herself shiver again.

She wondered what would happen if the crowds expressing their hatred of England knew that there were two English citizens in their midst.

Lord Wye must have had the same thought for he stopped whispering to her and, when they moved off, merely slouched along, dragging his feet a little as a man would do who was not quite certain what he was doing or where he was going.

They marched from dawn till nearly midday.

By that time many men from the forward columns had collapsed by the roadside, sitting down to rest and ease their aching feet or lying stretched out in utter exhaustion as the others moved slowly past them, making a jest or merely expressing their contempt of such weakness by a downturned thumb.

The ladies in the carriages drank wine, ate fruit and threw their empty bottles and their grape pips out of the windows. The mules bucked and the patient bullocks plodded on with their heavy wooden-wheeled carts creaking behind them.

At about noon the command came to halt.

The peasants flung themselves down at the side of the cart track, drew food of some sort or another from their pockets or scrounged behind the food carts, managing in some clever way of their own to filch a ration under the very noses of the Commissionaires.

The women were helped last, but they forced the Sergeants in charge to give them as much as they could spare and more, making every sort of excuse of sick or lame men, so that many of the soldiers obtained double rations and some even treble while others went short.

"Here, you share with us, *ma petite*," a bedraggled woman with a face like a gypsy and a baby strapped to her back said to Elvina. "Your man's in no fit state to fight for what he is entitled. You can pay me back when he gets his share tonight."

"Thank you," Elvina smiled.

The woman cooked some sort of concoction over a hastily lit fire. It looked disgusting, but it was at least eatable. Because Elvina and Lord Wye were hungry, they ate every scrap that was offered and wished for more.

Fires were forbidden on the march, but no one paid the least attention and only after an hour's cooking and eating did the Army resume its way up the hill.

The mules and bullocks were whipped to start them going, the muleteers yelling at them and at the men on the road to get out of their way. The gun carriages had to be pushed by a dozen men before the wretched animals dragging them could get them under way.

They were by now high up above the town.

They could see the little Harbour of St. Jean de Luz lying below them. In the blue sea beyond there were many ships and Elvina was sure that they all flew the English flag.

She felt Lord Wye press her arm.

"Was there ever such accursed luck as to be cast away on that particular sandbank?" he asked. "A little further down the coast and we would have been rescued by the Royal Navy."

"As it is we shall be rescued by the Army," she answered him.

He took her hand, squeezed it, and then continued to hold it in his, helping her up the hill for all that he seemed to be walking in so slipshod a fashion that anyone watching would have believed that she was assisting him.

They walked for another four hours until so many men seemed to be straggling behind that even the Marshal must have noticed the discrepancy in his ranks. But somehow they reached the top of the hill and had gone a little way down on the other side before the order was given to camp. _

From here they could look down into the rough undulating valley that rose into a tangle of mountains.

The woman who had cooked for them at midday suggested that they should place themselves near to her, but Lord Wye and Elvina moved away into the shelter of a rock.

There were people all round them and yet, at the same time, they had a little privacy, for the rock was on a ledge and it was impossible for anyone to approach them unseen.

Now they could talk so long as they did so in whispers and when possible in French.

"Your accent is bad," Elvina whispered, "but even so, an English word would sound strange coming from a French soldier. It is wiser to speak French just in case we are overheard."

Lord Wye nodded.

"I am worried about you," he said in French. "You must be very tired."

"There are many who are more tired still," she replied. "Think of those who have fallen out."

"The poor devils have very likely walked from Paris behind the Marshal," Lord Wye reflected. "Napoleon cannot have many men left if this is the best he can send against Wellington."

There was a note of elation in his voice that made Elvina say quickly,

"Hush! You sound too bright and gay – to be a man suffering from the effects of a head wound."

"By the way that gash in my forehead is throbbing abominably."

She took the bandage off and looked at it. It was slightly inflamed, but there was nothing she could do but bathe it and bandage it up again.

Lord Wye rose to go and collect his ration.

"Don't speak," Elvina begged of him. "Just stand round the cart until someone serves you."

He was away a long time and she grew anxious. She wondered if she should go in search of him, but was afraid of drawing the authorities' attention to Lord Wye.

Suppose, she reasoned, they felt him too incapable to go further and commanded him to return to the town.

Finally he appeared carrying a meagre ration of meat and bread.

"I was worried," Elvina whispered as he sank down beside her and they both started to eat.

"There was little left," he replied. "As usual the graft and greed of the men at the base endangers the fighting soldiers' lives more effectively than any bullets from the enemy."

He spoke bitterly and Elvina said wonderingly,

"Do you mind how much French soldiers suffer?"

"They are still human beings with empty bellies."

Elvina sat considering this, her little face serious and Lord Wye smiled at her expression.

"You must learn not to hate, Imp," he said.

"I know it's wrong," Elvina replied. "But the French have been so cruel and brutal that it is hard to think of them as ordinary men."

She shivered at the memory of the atrocities committed by Napoleon's Army.

Lord Wye put his arm around her.

"Let's sleep while we can. Come close to me, you are tired. It is warm now, but it will be cold before dawn. We are a good deal higher up than we were last night."

He pulled his blanket from his pack. It was threadbare from long usage, but it still had a little warmth in it.

He tucked it round Elvina.

"I shall be warm enough," she murmured drowsily.

He looked down at her face lying against his shoulder, her eyelids drooping with exhaustion. Her body was so thin and so light that he could hardly feel its weight against him.

"It's an adventure, is it not, Elvina?" he asked. "And I could not have managed it without you."

"I will look after you," she said indistinctly, her voice fading away into the dreams that were changing reality into fantasy.

Lord Wye smiled above her head.

If anyone had told him a week ago, he thought to himself, that he would be relying on a little, ragged Portuguese child for help, that he would be in the midst of the enemy Army, dressed in their uniform and under the leadership of Napoleon's most able and virile Marshal, he would have thought them demented.

He looked round at the men camped out the side of the mountain and thought that all Armies were much the same when they were not fighting.

Off duty the soldier was only a man who was hungry and tired, who wanted to laugh, drink and make love.

Not far away there was a crowd of soldiers and their women singing round a fire.

They had a bottle of wine between them and were passing it from hand to hand, each man taking his share and no more, each man, for a moment, content with the comradeship of his countrymen and a full stomach.

Lord Wye gave a little sigh.

The friendliness he sensed amongst those men was one of the reasons why he had begged the Prime Minister to let him join the Duke of Wellington's Army, even if only for a little while.

It was a friendliness that he could never feel at Carlton House and was something he often found lamentably lacking in the salons of the great London hostesses and even in the exclusive and select Clubs that he frequented.

Elvina stirred suddenly and gave a little cry and his arm tightened around her.

"What is it?" he asked.

"Don't hit me – please," she whimpered and then awoke with a start as Lord Wye's hand covered her mouth.

"You are speaking English."

"I am sorry," she whispered. "I was having a nightmare. I thought – I thought that my stepmother was about to – beat me."

"She shall never do it again," Lord Wye said. "You are away from her now."

"You will never send me back – you promise me that?" Elvina asked. "Even – even if we have to go to England via Lisbon?"

It was a fear that had been lurking at the back of her mind all day. She had been working out what would happen when they did reach the Duke of Wellington – if they did so. She guessed then there was every likelihood of Lord Wye being sent to Lisbon to find a ship to take him to England.

It was then that she thought of herself and how, once he was among his own people, Lord Wye might no longer wish to carry her to England.

He did not speak and she said, looking up at him and with one hand holding the lapel of his coat,

"Promise me! Promise me – that you will still take me with you – and that you will not leave me behind."

"Do you really trust me so little?" he asked. "I have given you my word because you have saved my life. Do you think I would go back on it?"

"N-no."

"I have made myself responsible for you and, God willing, we will both land in England together."

She felt the tears come into her eyes at the relief that swept over her. She had not even realised in that moment how afraid she had been.

"Thank you," she whispered. "Thank you. *Thank you.*"

She could see in the light of the fire the sudden look of tiredness in his face.

Because somehow his kindness was overwhelming, she hid her face against him.

"Poor little imp."

She heard his voice above her.

"It ought to have been so easy to take you to England and now I have got you into this mess."

"It is not – your fault," Elvina murmured.

"I am afraid I am responsible. If I had not been in such a hurry, if I had listened to the Captain, pray Heaven he has escaped, poor man, and the others on board."

"At least they had – money," Elvina said consolingly. "Being a prisoner is not so bad if you can pay the guards. The gold you have given your men will give them a great many luxuries – so long as it lasts."

"The War itself will not last long," Lord Wye said.

"How can you be sure of that?" Elvina asked.

"I am certain of it," Lord Wye replied. "This is the Emperor's last throw and the dice are loaded against him."

Elvina gave a little sigh and snuggled a little closer. She felt his encircling arm about her holding her comfortably as she drifted once again into sleep.

Several times during the night she awoke, feeling cramped or else aroused by some noise from the camp.

Each time she found Lord Wye awake, his arm still supporting her, his eyes looking out from under his bandaged forehead over the men and women sleeping on the ground around them.

Once she asked him a little drowsily,

"Why – do you not sleep?"

"I don't want to miss anything," he answered. "Besides for a change *I* am looking after *you*."

*

Dawn found them both stiff and a little chilled. The skies were grey and there was a wind blowing in from the sea.

"It looks like rain," Lord Wye remarked.

A little later, in some manner of his own, he managed to procure a torn blanket, which he placed over her shoulders.

Elvina guessed that he had filched it from one of the several men around them who had collapsed entirely during the night and who were obviously intent on straggling back down the hill to St. Jean de Luz.

She herself found a water bottle abandoned a little further up the road and they filled it from a clear mountain stream and felt that they might be glad of it later on.

As the day advanced, they pushed through the baggage carts and the women and were now a little nearer to the marching soldiers.

They were climbing again up another hill and the word went round that they were heading for St. Jean Pied de Port, where they were to join General Ney's divisions who were bringing sixty-six guns.

All this information cheered the troops enormously and despite the hard walking there seemed to be a greater spirit of determination than there had been the day before. Batches of men burst into song and even good-humouredly jerked some of the stragglers to their feet and helped them on their way carrying their muskets.

"If we beat them at St. Jean," one of the women said in Elvina's hearing, "perhaps that will be the end of the War and we will be home before Christmas."

"You said that last year!" another woman commented.

"And the year before!" cried another.

"Well, this time I believe I am right," the first woman said defensively. "A gypsy read my fortune a few days ago and saw me in a house with a roof. That would be a change, I can tell you."

The women round her sighed and Elvina realised that more than anything else they longed for the security and comfort of being static and not having to be continuously on the move.

They had only been marching for a little while when the grey skies of the morning fulfilled their promise.

Rain began to fall, soaking everyone indiscriminately with the exception of the ladies in the carriages, who closed the windows.

"Are you cold?" Lord Wye asked Elvina.

"No, only wet," she answered.

They walked in silence as did nearly everyone else.

Elvina had hoped at first that it was only a shower, but the rain now began to fall in torrents and when a halt was called at midday it was difficult to find the way through the blinding rain to the food carts.

It was then that Lord Wye and Elvina learned that there was some confusion and difficulty over the food supplies.

Murmurs began immediately amongst the troops and an Officer finally appeared to explain what had happened.

"The Marshal has ordered you bread," he explained, "but it has not arrived from Bayonne. It should have met us here. You will have to manage with what you have until this evening."

There were murmurs and protestations, but the Officer galloped away. The soldiers, dripping and miserable, could only shout curses at his retreating back.

The women had a great deal more to say, but oaths supplied no one with nourishment. Hungry and resentful the Army moved on during the afternoon and late in the evening came into St. Jean Pied de Port.

It was only a small town and it was already overcrowded with troops, but, even so, Elvina and Lord Wye learned that a great many more were expected.

"The bridge over the Nive at Cambo has gone," a soldier told a woman near them, "and the food carts cannot get through."

There was a scream of rage and anger at this and Elvina saw that the men and women around them were glancing at the houses, wondering if there was anything left to sack.

The Army pillaged the French towns and villages as pitilessly as those of Spain. Colonels who carried with them baggage trains of thirty vehicles containing plunder and women were hardly in a position to reprove soldiers who wished to help themselves to luxuries.

Indeed they did not attempt it, but it was obvious even to a stranger like Lord Wye that the Army was demoralised.

An advance guard of General Ney's soldiers came into the town almost simultaneously with the Division that Lord Wye and Elvina were a part of.

"We have been without food for two days," they shouted. "Give us somethin' to eat."

"The food carts are here!" someone cried.

There was a general surge forward, everyone squelching through the mud, pushing and fighting, soldiers even throwing their muskets away in their anxiety to reach the carts that were coming slowly down the narrow streets.

"Bread! Give us bread!" the women cried and rushed forward.

And then a roar of fury went up.

"What is the matter?" Elvina asked.

Lord Wye, almost carrying her, had managed to wedge himself against a doorway two steps above the crowd.

Although there was no protection from the rain, they were at least not in danger of being knocked down by the jostling fighting troops and their women.

"I cannot see," he answered. "Oh, now I realise what is the matter."

"What is it?"

"The carts contain flour," he answered. "They had hoped for bread, but there is only flour in the carts that have got through."

"Well, they can bake some bread," Elvina said practically.

"They are not going to get the chance,"

Lord Wye could see over the heads of the crowd and the women shaking their fists at soldiers slitting open the sacks. Senior-ranking Officers were giving orders, but no one was listening to them.

"It's wet! Soaked! Useless!"

The words swept round the town. There were more troops coming into the market place and they too started to shout.

"What is the use of wet flour? Feed it to the ducks!" a woman screamed and the soldiers took up the cry.

"Feed it to the ducks! We want bread! Feed it to the ducks!"

It looked as if the whole thing would turn into a riot and Elvina held tightly onto Lord Wye's arm. The flour that had come such a long way over the muddy roads was being thrown about.

A Sergeant took a handful straight in his face and another man, attempting to grab some, had his hand lashed with a musket and the blood gushed out, mingling with the sodden mass of flour and water and making the crowd cry out even more derisively that they were being deliberately starved.

Fighting began in one corner of the market place and then suddenly a cry went up.

"The oxen! Get to the oxen!"

There was a surge forward and even as the crowd began to take the patient beasts from between the shafts, Marshal Soult, surrounded by half a dozen Officers and a large number of mounted troops, came hurrying into the market place.

The men who were unfastening the oxen were beaten off by force.

"There will be hundreds of them outside the town!" someone shouted.

"I will shoot the first man who lays a hand on my animals!" Marshal Soult roared. "Listen to me, you fools. The oxen we have here in St. Jean have been assembled to drag our guns to the summit of Roncesvalles. That is where we are going to meet the British and beat them."

He slashed at a soldier near him with his sword.

"Do you want to fight without guns? Do you want to die merely because you cannot wait to fill your bellies? Fools! Idiots! *Dolts!* Life is more important than your own greed."

His great raucous voice seemed to echo round the whole market place. The contempt and anger in his tone silenced those who were complaining.

"Food is on its way," he went on. "Only the rain has prevented it from getting here. Other carts are at this very moment entering the town. Wait! Be patient. And you will all be fed."

He placed a guard round the bullock carts and galloped away. The soldiers cursed, but turned their attention to the houses, most of which were barricaded as if against the enemy,

"They are so used to sacking any place they go to," Lord Wye whispered to Elvina. "The fact that this is French territory is not going to stop them. Unfortunately for them, I doubt if there is much left."

Men began breaking down doors with the butts of their muskets. Others waited sullenly until another bullock cart appeared and then fought for the food it contained.

It was all indescribable confusion. As the carts came into the town some received two days' food, others got none. A dozen troopers defied all orders and in an obscure cul-de-sac roasted an ox whole, only allowing others to participate when they had gorged themselves.

By this time Lord Wye and Elvina had moved away from the crowded square and found shelter in the outhouse of a deserted mansion.

It must once have been a tool shed. There were still a few implements lying about and there were dry leaves on the floor.

"This will make a softer bed – than we had last night," Elvina cried.

"I will go and find something to eat," Lord Wye suggested. "Things should be quieter soon."

Elvina sprang to her feet.

"No, no. Don't leave me. I shall be – afraid."

"That I would not come back?" he asked.

"Anything might happen to you," she said. "You might be killed – or worse still discovered."

"At the same time we don't want to starve to death," he answered.

"We shall not. We are more fortunate than those who came from Bayonne. We have at least – eaten this morning.'

"All the same I could do with something this evening and so could you."

"Let me try," she begged. "Give me the francs that are left. I will go to one of the houses in a side street."

"I will come with you," he insisted firmly.

"No, I think I shall do better alone. People are afraid of, soldiers in this town and it's not surprising."

"I will not let you go without me," he went on.

She remembered then the drunken revellers in St. Jean de Luz and knew what he feared for her.

"Very well. But keep out of sight for I cannot believe that there is any patriotism left – only a hatred of war."

They went out again into the pouring rain. The street was deserted, but they could hear shouts and yells and not far away there was a golden glow in the sky as if a fire had started.

Elvina knocked on the door of four houses without avail.

At the fifth a voice asked,

"Who is there?"

"A child," Elvina replied.

"A child?" the voice questioned.

"Yes, a child," Elvina repeated. "No one else. I promise you."

She signalled to Lord Wye to keep in the shadows. The door was opened a crack and she saw that an elderly woman stood there, shading a taper with her hand.

"I have money, *madame*," Elvina said, "but I am starved. The soldiers have taken everything. There is nothing left in the town."

"I have nothin'," the woman answered and went to shut the door.

"Please, *madame*, please! For the love of God give me something to eat!" Elvina cried.

There was a moment's pause, a murmur of voices inside the house, as if someone protested, and then the woman thrust a piece of bread and a few potatoes into Elvina's hand.

"It's all I have," she replied. "No, I don't want money. Go away, child, for fear someone should see you and others come beggin'."

"Merci bien, madame! Merci! Merci!" Elvina cried.

She and Lord Wye hurried back to the safety of their tool shed.

The bread was not fresh, but it tasted like ambrosia. The potatoes seemed to Elvina to be as delicious as the first strawberries of the year.

They ate slowly, not talking, savouring every bite.

And when they had finished, Elvina gave a little sigh of satisfaction.

"That's better," she said. "But you are so big. It is very little for a man."

"Tomorrow we will find something better," Lord Wye said.

There was not much conviction in his tone.

"The baggage carts have arrived," Elvina said confidently. "The Marshal cannot let his Army starve."

"It would be irony indeed if to escape imprisonment we were to die of starvation," Lord Wye pointed out.

"We will not do that," Elvina answered. "Tomorrow I will beg again before we start the march to Roncesvalles.

Now let's sleep. But first – turn your back as I take off my wet gown. It will dry before the morning."

"What are you going to wear?" he enquired.

"Can I have the blanket from your pack?" she suggested.

"It is as wet as I am."

She looked round the tool shed. In a corner she saw something lying on a shelf. She pulled it down.

It was a long piece of sacking such as a gardener might use to collect leaves. It smelt of the earth and, when she shook it, some withered roots fell to the floor, but at least it was dry.

"Here is a beautiful nightgown," she laughed. "Now turn your back, my Lord."

He did as he was told and she slipped off her gown and hung it up from the roof so that it could drip on to the floor.

"The Duke of Wellington's letters are safe," she said, "but the ink may have run."

"They will be a bit out of date by the time we get home," Lord Wye said gloomily. "Perhaps it would be best to destroy them."

"Not when I have carried them so far," Elvina answered.

She felt suddenly gay and almost happy. They were out of the rain, they had eaten. Although the tool shed was dark, with only a light coming through the dirty windows from the glow outside, they were at least alone and sheltered from the crowds.

"We have not long to sleep," Elvina said. "Did you hear the Officer saying that we were to be ready to leave at – four o'clock in the morning?"

"Soult is driving his men hard," Lord Wye remarked. "If only we could get a word through to Wellington of the condition they are in."

"It may also be the same for the British Army," Elvina suggested practically.

"I cannot believe they are in the mess that this rabble has got itself into," Lord Wye said contemptuously.

Elvina wrapped herself in the sacking and sat down on the floor.

"You can turn round now," she told him.

Lord Wye rose to his feet and started to take off his coat.

"You are wet," Elvina remarked. "I suppose we could not make a fire and get our clothes dry?"

"It is too difficult in this ramshackle place," he answered. "We should burn it down and then there would be nothing for it but the rain. Listen to it now on the roof."

It seemed as if it would never stop raining, beating down relentlessly.

"No, I suppose you are right. I expect we shall both have colds and that will be extremely unpleasant."

"I have a sore throat already," Lord Wye grumbled. "I cannot think why you are not dead, with what you have been through."

"I am tough."

"You don't look it," he answered.

He suddenly put out his hands towards her.

"Only a child," he said, "and yet you have the courage of a lion and the strength of ten men. As I told you last night, this is an adventure, but, God knows, I feel scared at times."

Elvina put her hands out to him as he sat down beside her on the floor.

"It is getting dark," he said, "and I can hardly see you, but I know that you are there and it matters a lot. Are you glad of that?"

Elvina felt a sudden constriction in her heart because of the almost caressing note in his voice and the strength of his fingers on hers and the fact that he was very near to her. Quite unexpectedly she felt shy.

"Of – of course I am – glad," she answered and it was difficult to force the words between her lips.

Lord Wye released her hands and rolled onto his back, moving his shoulders amongst the leaves to make himself comfortable.

"Funny little imp!" he chuckled. "Kiss me goodnight."

CHAPTER SEVEN

For Elvina the next three days passed in a kind of nightmare in which she marched and slept and marched again until she was past thinking of anything except the effort of putting one foot in front of the other.

At times she felt that she could go no farther and that she must drop out as so many of the soldiers were doing.

She passed them lying in crumpled heaps on the mountainside, their eyes closed in the sleep of utter exhaustion that no longer could be denied.

Only the fact that Lord Wye was beside her kept her going. She clung to him and he pulled her along the rough stony roads where Marshal Soult's columns, strung out like heavily moving snakes, had no room to deploy.

"I will carry you," he said more than once, but she shook her head.

"If you are well enough to carry me," she whispered, "you will be well enough to face the English in the front line."

Actually, while Elvina scented danger around them all the time, those who marched beside them had little thought except for their own misery and discomfort.

The men cursed and many of the women wept, yet still they went on, climbing all the time towards the summit of the mountains where they had learned that by now the British had their outposts.

Elvina, with her aching legs and bleeding feet, had no interest in the strategy that she knew Lord Wye was considering.

Despite his habitual look of semi-consciousness he was taking in every detail of the mountainous terrain and missing nothing of the conversation around them.

The Officers, obviously under Marshal Soult's orders, galloped up and down the lines trying to infuse some enthusiasm into the troops.

"We shall be in Roncesvalles by tomorrow!" they shouted. "There will be food there, food and wine and women! Get a move on if you want to enjoy yourselves."

Their exhortations, all too familiar to the veterans, did little to relieve the general gloom and, when in the morning of the third day they were told to be ready to attack, there were only more grumbles than before and if possible less enthusiasm.

Officers ordered and bullied men at the rear of the columns into going forward. Scattering stones behind his horse, one galloped up to where Lord Wye and Elvina were resting.

"Get up to the front?" he called out roughly.

Lord Wye made no answer, merely sitting looking stupid, his musket held limply in his hands.

"It's no use, *monsieur*," Elvina said shrilly, speaking with a defiance that she had heard other women use. "He is still dazed and it's my belief the British bullet is still lodged in his head. The surgeons in the hospital had no more sense or knowledge than a new born babe."

Without wasting further words on what he sensed was a hopeless case, the Officer whirled his horse round and galloped on to find further stragglers.

"What do we do now?" Elvina asked.

"I don't know," Lord Wye answered, raising his head to search the top of the mountains.

It was incredibly tantalising to think that the British were so near and yet the whole front line of Marshal Soult's Army lay between them and the British outpost holding the Maya Pass.

Early in the afternoon heavy fire from the guns that had been dragged by the oxen into position seemed to shake the whole mountain.

As the first order to fire came, Elvina involuntarily threw herself against Lord Wye and clung to him, expecting the whole ground beneath them to dissolve in fire and smoke.

He held her tightly and then after a few minutes of the bombardment she raised her head.

"What is – happening?" she asked tremulously.

"It's difficult to see for the smoke," he replied.

The French had the initiative, but the British were prepared to answer back. Cannonballs began to fall among the forward line of troops and then some further back, falling amongst the peasants carrying the ammunition who promptly ran for their lives.

It was quite obvious from the noise itself that the British guns were outmatched, but still they went on firing although it was evident that nothing was to be achieved by mere gunfire.

The French guns now ceased firing and the order was given to advance. With their muskets raised the French infantry moved forward over the rocky ground.

From where Lord Wye and Elvina were resting amongst a crowd of women, baggage carts and peasants, it was easy to see what was happening along the whole mountainside.

Puffs of smoke were followed by the roar of the British cannon. The first line of the advancing troops fell. The remainder closed their ranks and went forward climbing steadily towards the summit.

"The British infantry are holding their fire," Lord Wye cried excitedly.

"Be careful," Elvina said.

She put a warning hand on his arm, for she had seen a woman turn her head as he spoke.

"The French troops are good and steady," Lord Wye whispered. "Let's pray our own are better."

The French columns had almost reached the top and now, amidst the fusillade of shot, they began to fall. Even above the noise of the gunfire they could hear the Officers yelling at the men, encouraging and exhorting them.

The advance continued despite the casualties. Men toppled over, but the ranks closed until suddenly the front line began to waver.

It was so strange to watch that one could hardly believe it was happening to real people, to flesh and blood.

A sudden hesitation on the part of the blue line, a wave of men falling to the ground in front of their advancing comrades, another line down and yet another.

And now the steadiness had gone, the attack had failed.

Soult's men were in retreat! They came back leaving two long lines of their dead and wounded stretched out upon the ground.

They came stumbling to where their womenfolk were waiting for them, some of them blinded by smoke, many bleeding in the head and arms. Many returned only to fall dying or dead even as they reached safety.

Elvina closed her eyes. She had always known that war was horrible, cruel and bestial, but she had not imagined that it could be like this.

She felt suddenly that she was going to faint as a man, his face shattered beyond recognition, collapsed in the road almost at their feet. She felt Lord Wye's hand come up and cover her eyes.

"Don't look," he murmured.

It was perhaps his kindness that broke the tension. She felt the tears running down her cheeks and could only gasp,

"It's horrible! Those men. Those poor men!"

"Think of our own soldiers!" Lord Wye suggested.

The Officers were rallying the troops. General d'Erlon, who commanded this particular section of the line, was having a hurried consultation only a short distance away from where Lord Wye sat holding Elvina in his arms.

"We have to take the pass," they heard him say. "The Marshal's orders. Tell the gunners to start again and keep going and get the men into some sort of order."

"There are quite a lot of casualties, *mon General*," one of his Lieutenants ventured.

"Would you lose Spain for a few casualties?" General d'Erlon asked sharply.

Some of the wounded dragged themselves to safety while others lay where they had fallen.

"Are they going to do it – all over again?" Elvina asked.

Striving to control her tears, trying not to look at the wounded who, bleeding and with shattered limbs, were being carried past them to the wooden wagons which would take them back to St. Jean Pied de Port.

Lord Wye did not answer and after a moment she raised herself within his encircling arm and looked to see what was occupying his attention.

"Is that smoke on the mountaintop?" she asked.

"I thought at first it was cloud," Lord Wye said. "But, by God, it is around us too. It is fog. Fog in July! Are there any limits to this extraordinary weather?"

By five o'clock that afternoon the fog was so dense that it was impossible to see more than a few feet around them. The attacks were called off and the soldiers were told to bivouac where they stood.

Lord Wye suddenly stood up.

"Come with me," he said to Elvina.

"Where to?" she enquired.

He took her by the hand and a squeeze on her fingers told her that he wanted her to ask no questions. They moved across the road and keeping to the right started walking over the scrub and heather.

"Where are you going?" someone asked out of the greyness.

"Is this the way to the food carts?" Elvina enquired quickly.

"*Hélas!* You will be fortunate indeed if you find a food cart," came the answer. "They never come anywhere where it's dangerous."

They moved on, still keeping to the right of the troops, Elvina thought, climbing all the time.

Soon they knew that they were in what had been the battlefield of a few hours earlier, for they came upon several dead men and heard people moving near them, although the fog seemed impenetrable.

Several dead soldiers had already been stripped of everything valuable and Elvina knew that the scavengers were at work.

These were the peasants, who were always on the field of battle before the firing had ceased and about whom many terrible stories were told.

Lord Wye gave her no time to worry about either the dead or the wounded.

Picking his way over the fallen bodies, he pulled Elvina with him until, standing on a stone, she gave a little whimper of pain.

It was then he bent down and picked her up in his arms.

"No – it's dangerous," she said hastily.

"Not in this fog," he answered. "We may be shot by our own side, but it is a chance we have to take."

"I can walk," she told him.

"You have walked far enough," he answered. "Put your arms around my neck."

She obeyed him and realised how strong he was and how easily he could carry her up the steep climb to the top of the mountain.

All the time he was bearing right, stopping every now and then to listen. It seemed to Elvina that everything about them was uncannily quiet.

There was only the damp cold fog and the beating of her own heart and Lord Wye's.

He was frightened too she thought. She could hear his heart throbbing beneath her breast, and suddenly she realised that she was no longer afraid, only content because he held her so close, because now at this moment the battle, the wounded and the long exhausting march seemed far away and forgotten.

It was just the two of them alone, lost in a No Man's Land between two opposing forces.

'Either side might open fire on us,' Elvina told herself, but thought, even so, that all her fears had left her.

She knew then, and it came as no surprise, that she loved the man who held her. She had known it, she thought, when she had bent to kiss him in that dark tool shed in St. Jean Pied de Port.

Later, while he slept, wrapped in the piece of sacking which smelt of the earth, she had lain awake.

'I am happy!' she thought and was astonished at how happy she was.

She knew now it was because he had been there beside her and once again she was ecstatically happy because he held her and because she felt safe.

No human beings could be in a more dangerous situation than they were at the moment, but nothing mattered except for Lord Wye's nearness and the haven in his arms.

'*I love him!*'

She almost said the words aloud and with a little sinking of her heart remembered that, if they reached safety, they would no longer be two people together surrounded by the enemy.

Lord Wye would be with his friends again, a Nobleman, a member of the Royal Household, and she – what would she be to him?

She had grown used to thinking of him as her own possession.

"Give this to your man," a woman had said, offering her a titbit from their meagre rations.

"Get your man out of the way!" the muleteers had shouted when a bullock cart wanted to pass them.

Soon he would no longer need her protection. The fear of the future made her tighten her arms around Lord Wye's neck. He bent his head suddenly and laid his cheek against hers.

"It's all right, child," he said soothingly.

'I am not afraid,' she wanted to tell him, but the words died in her throat for the sudden joy that shot through her at the touch of his cheek and the sound of his voice.

She wanted to turn her face a little and touch his lips with hers. She wanted to draw him even closer and then felt herself blush at the very audacity of her feelings.

Quite suddenly he put her down on the ground.

"What is – happening?" she asked.

"We crawl from here," he whispered. "And don't say anything. We must be near the British posts."

They went down on their hands and knees. Lord Wye kept hold of Elvina's hand, drawing her beside him up over the rough stones and clumps of heather.

She felt soon that her knees were bleeding and she could hear her skirt tearing as it was caught on a dried stick or a piece of bramble.

Quite suddenly there was the sound of voices.

Lord Wye raised his head and Elvina listened too.

There was no mistaking what they heard.

Although they could not quite distinguish the words, the tone was British.

"Help!" Lord Wye shouted in English. "Help!"

There was silence and he shouted again.

"*Help*!"

Not far away from them a rough voice came out of the fog, but it spoke the English tongue.

"Who be there?"

"An Englishman from the enemy's lines," Lord Wye answered.

"Come forward and let's 'ave a look at you," the voice commanded.

Elvina heard someone else say,

"Be careful, Jack, maybe 'tis a trap."

"It's no trap," Lord Wye shouted. "I am English."

He let go of Elvina's hand for a moment and she could feel him make a sudden movement.

She knew then that he was throwing off his coat.

"You will be cold," she said warningly.

"First impressions are often the most important," he said with a hint of laughter in his voice.

She knew that his eyes would be twinkling and she loved him more because he could still be amused in such a situation as this.

"I am coming towards you," Lord Wye shouted. "I have a child with me."

"If it's one of your damned tricks, you'll pay for it," a voice replied. "We dinna trust no Frenchies."

"I am not a Frenchy," Lord Wye replied.

He had taken Elvina's hand in his again and now they were going forward step by step. They must have reached the top of the mountain for it was terribly cold and now suddenly out of the gloom they could see two soldiers and both had muskets pointed at them.

"It is no trap," Lord Wye said quietly. "We are alone, as you see. I am Lord Wye, a member of the Royal Household. I wish to be taken immediately to your Commanding Officer."

"You speak as if you were one of us," one of the soldiers said.

"I am one, can you not tell that?" Lord Wye enquired.

"'Ere, let's get 'im into the light," the other sentry suggested.

He put his hand somewhat roughly on Lord Wye's shoulder, but the other said to Elvina,

"Hold on to me, little 'un. 'Tis rough goin' and you dinna want to be lost in this accursed fog."

They walked for some way and then suddenly there were camp fires, lights, soldiers in red tunics and Highlanders in their tartan kilts, all staring at them, it seemed to Elvina, as the two sentries marched Lord Wye into the light from the leaping flames of a fire.

"He be a Frenchy!" someone exclaimed. "Look at his breeches."

"Don't be a fool!" Lord Wye said and his voice was the firm calm voice of authority. "I told you I had come from the French lines. Take me to your Commanding Officer. It is urgent."

A Sergeant took charge.

"Back to your posts men," he said to the sentries.

"You were right to bring him in."

He looked at Elvina and then at Lord Wye.

"Any explanation as to why we should believe you?"

"The explanation I have will keep for your Commanding Officer," Lord Wye replied. "Now, do as you are told. There is no time to be lost."

The Sergeant was obviously impressed by his bearing for all that he looked wild and strange enough, Elvina thought, with his dirty shirt, bandaged head, torn breeches, Army boots and flapping gaiters.

She did not think of her own appearance until they were in Sir Rowland Hill's tent, drinking a glass of wine, which he had hastily poured for them.

"I can hardly believe it!" Sir Rowland was saying. "It's an incredible story. You have been in the French lines all these days and no one had any suspicion that you were English?"

"That was entirely thanks to Elvina," Lord Wye replied with a smile."

"This child?" Sir Rowland asked.

He looked at Elvina as if he had seen her for the first time.

It was then that she was suddenly conscious of how she must appear, with her dirty torn gown, her bare feet, a piece of rag tied over her hair and her skin dark not only from the walnut juice but also from the hot sun, the bitter winds and the soaking rain.

She had experienced them all in the last few days and each had left their mark.

"Wellington is not far away," Sir Rowland told Lord Wye, "You know, of course, that we are making an attack on San Sebastián?"

"No, I did not know it," Lord Wye said. "Will it fall, do you think?"

Sir Rowland Hill shrugged his shoulders,

"They have a strong force there. We can but hope."

"I must get to Wellington at once," Lord Wye said. "I have some idea of the strength of Marshal Soult's Army and I know that he intends to concentrate his attack on Roncesvalles."

"You will find him, I think, at Lesaca," Sir Rowland said. "It will be impossible for you to go tonight, my Lord, in this fog. But it should lift by the morning."

"I will leave at dawn,"

"And your companion?" Sir Rowland enquired.

Before Lord Wye could speak Elvina said quickly.

"I will go with you. You cannot leave me behind."

"She will come with me," Lord Wye said quietly. "Can you spare two horses?"

"Certainly, my Lord."

"Then we had best get a little sleep," Lord Wye said with a smile.

"I am afraid we have nothing very comfortable to offer you," Sir Rowland apologised.

"We are not used to comfort," Lord Wye answered. "But as it is cold, I should appreciate the loan of a coat."

"I have already given orders for a complete change of clothes. I am afraid that they will not be what your Lordship is accustomed to, but the best we can provide at a moment's notice."

*

It was indeed strange, Elvina thought at dawn, to see Lord Wye in the uniform of an Officer of the Light Dragoons. The gold epaulets, the coloured sash and the high peaked cap with its aigrette were extremely becoming.

"It's not a bad fit," he admitted with a smile.

"I am afraid we could not raise you beyond a Major's rank," Sir Rowland laughed. "You are too broad-shouldered for me and the trousers actually belong to some poor fellow who was sent to the base two days ago with a bullet through his shoulder.

"I will see that the clothes are returned with interest as soon as I reach England," Lord Wye said.

"It is a pleasure to be able to accommodate you," Sir Rowland answered.

Elvina had been provided with a Highlander's plaid to wear round her shoulders, but as she and Lord Wye rode away down the mountainside, the sun came out and it was warm enough in the valley for her to discard it.

They had an escort of three men with them and they were anxious to move with all haste away from the danger zone.

They rode hard and Elvina began to think that horse riding was even more exhausting than marching when one of their escort pointed ahead and hold them that the few roofs just coming into sight was the town of Lesaca.

"Thank the Lord we have not had to walk all this way," Lord Wye said to Elvina.

She gave him a doubtful little smile and he drew in his reins and asked,

"Are we going too fast for you? How damnably selfish I am. I had forgotten that you might not be as used to riding as I am."

"I have ridden," Elvina replied, "but not for some years. When her mother was alive, she had a pony, but Juanita had sold it a few weeks after she became my stepmother."

"I am sorry," Lord Wye said, suddenly contrite. "Why did you not tell me?"

"I am not tired," Elvina replied, "only a little stiff."

"If I had thought of it, I could easily have taken you in the front of my saddle. Can you manage this last mile or so?"

"Of course I can. We have been through worse, haven't we?"

It was an appeal, if he had but known it.

An appeal for him to remember what they had been through together. An appeal for him to go on remembering and not to abandon her, indeed not to draw away from her now that they were reaching security.

"Much worse," he smiled.

They rode into Lesaca to find that the Duke of Wellington had set up his Headquarters in the Town Hall. They hurried there and Elvina knew by the eagerness with which Lord Wye dismounted that he was longing to see the Commander-in-Chief.

The sentry, smart in his movements although his dress was soiled and faded as if he had been in many battles, led them down a corridor to what, before the event of war, had been the Mayor's parlour.

An *aide-de-camp*, hearing who they were, left them for a few minutes.

Lord Wye looked at Elvina.

"You are now going to see a man who, in my opinion, is one of the greatest Generals that the British Army has ever known," he said.

"Can he really beat Marshal Soult?" she asked. "Think how many men he had. Think of all those guns – and they are fighting in their own country."

"Marshal Soult is already beaten," Lord Wye told her quietly.

Elvina turned her back suddenly and drew from her breast the dispatches that had lain there since Lord Wye first entrusted them to her.

She looked at them with dismay. Crumpled and creased, the rain had reduced them to little more than pulp and the writing that was left was undecipherable.

She held them out to Lord Wye without a word.

He took them from her with a tender smile on his lips and would have spoken only the door opened and he turned his head eagerly.

"The Commander-in-Chief will see you now, my Lord," an *aide-de-camp* said.

They walked past him and into the room beyond, the Duke of Wellington was standing in what had been the Council Chamber. A slight, upright wiry-looking man with keen grey eyes and a large aquiline nose.

After Marshal Soult and other Generals whom Elvina had seen he was extraordinarily unostentatious. He wore a blue frock coat, dirty and stained with mud, a small crested cocked hat without feathers, a short cape and strapped grey trousers.

He stepped forward with outstretched hand.

"This is a great surprise. Lord Wye," he said. "I believed you to be on your way home carrying my dispatches to the Prime Minister."

"I should have been there by now," Lord Wye replied, "except for the most unfortunate contretemps. I should like to tell your Lordship about it, but may I first present the lady to whom I owe my presence here at this moment. And incidentally my life?"

Elvina dropped a deep curtsey. The Duke bowed and she saw the astonishment in his eyes as he looked at her torn dirty gown beneath a Highlander's plaid.

"You have undoubtedly had some very strange adventures, my Lord," he said to Lord Wye. "Will you tell me about them?"

"More important than my adventures," Lord Wye replied, "is the information I think I can give you about Marshal Soult's Army."

"That should be interesting," the Duke said.

He sat down at a table, chairs were brought by an *aide-de-camp* for Lord Wye and Elvina, a map was put between them and Lord Wye began to relate what had happened after they had escaped from the French Commodore at St. Jean de Luz and joined the French Army.

The Duke of Wellington said very little. He followed their route on the map and made a few noises of approval in his throat when Lord Wye described the attack of the day before and how Sir Rowland Hill's men had repulsed it.

He had just begun to ask questions when a messenger, dusty and with beads of sweat on his forehead, came hurrying into the room.

"From Roncesvalles, my Lord," he said, holding out a dispatch.

Lord Wellington took it quickly.

"Two Battalions of the seventh Division commanded by Brigadier Barnes report some success against the French in the Bastion," he said and there was a sudden gleam in his eyes although the tone of his voice held little emotion.

"Oh, I am glad!" Elvina exclaimed. "But the French have so many guns!"

The Duke did not appear to have heard her. It was obvious that his mind was preoccupied with his Armies.

Lord Wye rose to his feet.

"Is there some way of getting me to the coast, my Lord?" he asked.

The Duke turned to his *aide-de-camp*.

"See that Lord Wye is conveyed to Santander," he said.

"Thank you, my Lord," Lord Wye answered.

They shook hands and Elvina curtseyed and, even as they left the room, they heard the Duke ordering his horse to be saddled immediately.

Food and drink was provided for them and fresh horses and then they set forth over the Cantabrian Mountains towards Santander.

It was strange to find this rather barren part of the coast thick with British troops marching up towards the front line, bivouacking on the way, playing games when they were not required to be on the move and altogether making themselves at home in what was normally a very desolate part of the country.

The Duke of Wellington had, however, improved the roads and after a good night's rest in a small village, Elvina did not find the ride so hard as she had the journey the day before.

What was more Lord Wye was considerate and insisted on taking a rest every now and then, while members of their escort went ahead and arranged their accommodation for the night, so that when they arrived at a stopping place they found everything prepared for them.

Elvina managed to clean herself up and even in one place to buy from the proprietor's daughter of the inn where they slept a clean square of muslin to cover her head.

It was not until they arrived in Santander that Lord Wye remembered that, while he had been fitted out anew, she was literally in rags.

"Is there anywhere in the town where we can buy clothes, ladies' clothes?" he asked the young Lieutenant who was in charge of their escort.

"I should think so, my Lord," the Lieutenant replied. "When I arrived here from England, I thought the girls looked rather attractive, but I did not stay long enough to find out."

He must have impressed the innkeeper with Lord Wye's importance because shopkeepers arrived only too willing to sell bales of material, shawls and ribbons.

"Buy what you want," Lord Wye told her.

Elvina looked at him enquiringly.

"Do you really mean that?" she asked. "Perhaps it would be best if you could tell me how much you would wish to spend. I should not wish to be extravagant."

"I think the gold that I carry with me and which you have never allowed me to spend will be enough to fit you out," he smiled. "If not, I assure you that my credit is good enough to enable me to borrow all I require from the Army Paymaster who, I am sure, can be found somewhere in the town."

Still Elvina hesitated.

It was hard to believe that she was really, for the first time for six years, to have new clothes. And then caution told her that these things might look very shabby in England.

What was the fashion in some obscure town in Spain was not likely to seem the latest mode in Bond Street.

Accordingly she bought two lengths of muslin, a soft warm shawl, some ribbons and a little chip straw bonnet that she felt was more necessary than ornamental.

She noticed that morning when she dressed herself that the dye that she had darkened her hair with was either wearing off or had been washed off by the rains.

The gold was showing through and she knew that unless she could procure some more dye there was every likelihood that before she reached England she would be fair.

Lord Wye paid for the clothes she had chosen, throwing a couple of guineas to the shopkeepers who received them with delight, bowing and scraping their way from the room.

"Thank you! *Thank you!*" Elvina enthused.

He stood looking down at her and then, suddenly, his hand went out to cup her chin and tip her face up to his.

"You are such a child," he said quietly, "to be so pleased with a few scraps of muslin and a ribbon or two when you have done so much for me. How can I ever reward you, little Elvina, can you tell me that?"

"I want – no reward," she answered.

And then, although she tried to prevent herself saying it, it came from between her lips.

"All I want is to stay with you – not to leave you."

The words were passionate, spoken from the very depths of her heart.

He smiled down at her, the affectionate smile of a brother.

"I shall look after you, I swear to you. But I cannot promise that we can always be together."

"But that is what I want," Elvina said. "To be with you, as we have been these past days."

"You will think differently when you reach England."

He released her and walked across to the window. Outside there was a view of the Harbour, which was filled with naval vessels of all sorts, all flying the British flag.

"We shall soon be in England," he said jubilantly.

His words struck Elvina like a blow because she knew, as clearly as if she had heard him say it, that when they reached England she would lose him.

CHAPTER EIGHT

Elvina stared at herself in the looking glass and felt her spirits drop.

She had been so excited about her new gowns and she had watched the seamstress carefully sew the material that Lord Wye had bought her.

She had chosen the ribbons and the lining and had been willing to be fitted not once but a dozen times.

She could not remember when she had last had a new dress. The only clothes she had ever had to wear were old things of Juanita's that she was bored with.

To have something of her own and to be given the choice of materials was something so exciting that she could hardly believe it was true until she slipped the gown over her head, let the seamstress fasten it and turned to look at herself in the mirror.

It was then that she realised how very little difference it made to her appearance.

Owing to the hard marching, sleeping out of doors and the very scanty rations that she and Lord Wye had existed on, she was thinner than ever.

What was more, the darkness of her skin, with sunburn superimposed on the walnut juice, gave her an almost unpleasant swarthiness, which was somehow unnatural and without the moist bloom that existed on a naturally dark skin.

Her hazel eyes, too big for her face, stared back at her and filled with tears. She had believed that she would look so different.

She had imagined herself fair and pretty with a white skin against the soft muslin of the gown and it was like a blow to realise that she looked almost grotesque.

"The Señorita is pleased?" the seamstress asked.

"Yes, yes, of course," Elvina answered, knowing that it was not the woman's fault that she looked so strange.

The gown fitted her with the skirt falling gracefully from the high waist. But above the waist there was only flatness and a lack of curves.

'No one will ever suspect me of being anything but a child,' Elvina thought ruefully.

She no longer worried that her hair was beginning to lose its dye. No one was likely to look at her or indeed suspect that she was anything but what she appeared.

The sewing woman had trimmed the chip bonnet for day wear and she had a little wreath of flowers and ribbons to wear in the evening which would prevent anyone looking too closely and noting where the gold was supplanting an artificial darkness.

"Shall I finish the other gowns now?" the seamstress asked, interrupting Elvina's thoughts.

"Yes, yes, please do."

She turned from the mirror to go downstairs. She had thought to run down, gay-hearted and excited, and surprise Lord Wye with her appearance.

Now she knew that she did not really wish him to look at her but to remember her as she had been when they trudged together side by side away from St. Jean de Luz, when she had slept close beside him in the heather or when he had carried her close against his heart through the fog.

'Never again! Never again!'

The words seemed to echo in her mind and memories of what had been and what lay ahead had kept her awake last night when she had slept between sheets in the comfortable inn at Santander.

As soon as dawn broke she had gone to the window and seen the line of troops, the supply wagons and the guns coming from the quay and moving away through the town towards the mountains where the Duke of Wellington awaited them.

She watched them pass with envy in her eyes. How she wished she could be going with them! If only she and Lord Wye could join the newly disembarked troops.

If only they had not to take a ship for England.

Once she had longed to go to England with an intensity that had supplanted everything else in her mind.

Now she wanted only one thing – to remain with the man she loved.

It was agony to think that the minutes were ticking past and that they had only a very short time left together.

Elvina knew little of Society and its ways, but she was quite certain that once Lord Wye was back with his own people, surrounded with all the trappings and pomposity of his position, he would seem a very different person.

"When you are hungry," a soldier had once said to her when she was talking with him in the hospital in Lisbon, "a man's rank and his position cease to count."

She knew the truth of that. She remembered the potatoes that Lord Wye and she had devoured in St. Jean Pied de Port. She could see him now savouring every mouthful and then licking his fingers at the end like a child.

They had laughed about it and he had said,

"I would rather have eaten those at this moment than a dozen banquets in the past."

"Could you manage some more?" Elvina had asked, teasing him.

"A sackful," he replied, "and then I should still be hungry!"

On the march they had fought for the tough meat that was doled out from the food carts and had been so hungry that they had hardly waited until it was properly cooked before stuffing it into their mouths.

While the bread, which had been black and heavy so that many of the troops had grumbled and complained about it, seemed to them like manna to the Israelites of old.

How different it was going to be in England!

Elvina walked down the oak stairs of the inn slowly, reluctant for Lord Wye to see her and yet at the same time eager to be with him again.

She had reached the door of the private sitting room that had been allotted to them when she heard voices inside.

'Who could be with Lord Wye?' she wondered.

Then suddenly the door opened and she found herself face to face with a strange young man.

"Excuse me," he said and opened the door wider for her to pass through.

Over his head Elvina could see Lord Wye standing by the mantelshelf and talking to a woman. She saw his face, animated and amused, his eyes alight, his lips smiling.

Then she moved forward, a sudden heavy constriction within her chest and a sudden tightening within her throat.

She had reached Lord Wye's side before he seemed to realise that she was there.

Then he turned to her and put his arm around her shoulders.

"I was just thinking of you," he said. "In fact I had asked Mister Howard to go in search of you."

Elvina wanted to answer and wanted to ask who Mister Howard was, but she had eyes only for the woman who faced her. Never had she seen anyone so attractive, so fashionable or so overwhelming in every way.

Dark flashing eyes with dark curls framing a magnolia skin and a mouth as red as ripe cherries. She was fascinating, whoever she might be and Elvina knew, as surely as if someone had told her so, dangerous.

"Lady Cleone, may I present Elvina, who, as I have already told you, has saved my life?"

"What a charming child!" Lady Cleone said in what Elvina knew to be an affected voice. "And how clever of her to be so useful to you."

"Useful is hardly the word," Lord Wye answered. "A Guardian Angel is perhaps more appropriate."

"A very dark one," Lady Cleone said with a little sidelong glance of her eyes.

Lord Wye's arm tightened round Elvina's shoulders. At the same time he laughed and Elvina felt her face burn with anger and resentment.

She managed to make a small curtsey and then heard Lord Wye say as he turned her round towards the young man who had opened the door and who was now coming towards them,

"And this, Elvina, is Lady Cleone's brother, Peregrine Howard."

"I thought this must be the young lady I was seeking," the Honourable Peregrine Howard smiled.

"It is indeed," Lord Wye nodded. "And now I must offer you both a glass of wine."

"No, no," Lady Cleone replied. "I feel we have no time for it. There is so much to be done if we are to sail this evening. There are a dozen things I must buy in the town if it is possible to buy anything in such a benighted spot."

"It depends what you require," Lord Wye said.

"I will not bore you with a recitation of them, but I shall look forward to greeting you this evening, my Lord, and let's pray we have a pleasant voyage."

"It is most kind of you to invite us," Lord Wye replied.

He hurried forward to escort Lady Cleone and her brother to the door. He held her small grey-gloved hand for what seemed to Elvina an unconscionable time before he raised it to his lips and then, with a little coquettish smile from under her feather-trimmed bonnet and a rustle of her silk-lined skirts, Lady Cleone was gone.

"That is indeed fortunate," Lord Wye said, coming back to the sitting room where Elvina awaited him.

"What is?" she asked in a voice that even to herself sounded cold and far away.

"A frigate is carrying Lady Cleone and her brother back from Sicily where their father, the Earl of Severn, is commanding our Expeditionary Force. They have invited us to join them and I have accepted with much gratitude."

"Why?" Elvina asked.

"Why!" Lord Wye questioned with raised eyebrows. "Because, my dear child, we shall be much more comfortable and our passage to England will be much swifter. A troop ship, in which I had expected we should make the voyage, would be excessively slow. What is more I think that you and I have roughed it for quite long enough. We shall find everything we need abroad the frigate."

'We shall also find Lady Cleone,' Elvina longed to say.

But because she was too afraid to put her thoughts into words she could only turn away from him and walk towards the window.

"It will be good to be in England again," Lord Wye went on. "At the same time already I am feeling a little sorry our adventure is over, aren't you, Elvina?"

"Is it – over?" she asked in a curiously flat tone.

"No, I forgot. For you it is only just beginning. You are going to join your sister in England. You are going to start a new life in a new country. For me it will be a case of taking up life where I left it."

He stretched himself.

"Ah, well! I have certainly learned to appreciate a comfortable bed. Those nights on the mountain were hardly one's idea of being comfortable."

"Yet they were fun – were they not?" Elvina queried.

Before he could answer she turned from the window and went towards him.

"You will not forget me. *Promise* me you will not – forget me."

There was an intensity and a plea in her voice.

But he did not seem to hear it.

"Good gracious!" he exclaimed. "I did not notice when you came into the room. You have on a new gown! That was most remiss of me. Let me look at you."

"No, no, don't look at me," Elvina said. "I look – horrible. I should not have chosen white muslin. It was stupid of me."

"You are getting fashion conscious, are you?" he asked with a little note of laughter in his voice. "Oh, Elvina, don't grow up too quickly. Remain a child. You will be far happier that way."

"Why do you think that?" she enquired.

"Because," he answered, "once you are grown up you will be embroiled in the intrigues of your heart. You will either be in love with someone who is not in love with you or you will be bored with someone who is lovesick for a look from your eyes. Either way you will be a dead bore. Stay as you are, that is how I like you."

With an effort that was almost superhuman Elvina forced a smile to her lips.

"If that is how – you want me," she said, "I will remain young. I will not grow any older."

"That is right," he laughed. "Thirteen years of age for ever. We will drink a toast to it, shall we?"

He turned from the mantelshelf and pulled the bell pull. They heard the bell clang far away somewhere in the bowels of the inn.

"A toast," Lord Wye repeated, "to Elvina the brave, to little Portugal and *damnation* to Napoleon's Armies."

He crossed to the window to watch a detachment of troops passing in the street below and Elvina followed him.

Suddenly she slipped her small thin fingers into his hand.

"Let's go with them," she whispered. "Let's go back to fight beside the Duke of Wellington. You would like that – I know. The British are advancing and soon they will be over the mountains and into France, driving towards Paris and defeating the Emperor with every step they make. Let's go – with them."

She felt Lord Wyc's fingers tighten over hers and knew that he was listening to what she was saying, following in his mind the British reinforcements.

For a moment she knew that he was tempted. For a moment she even thought that he might agree to her suggestion.

And then he released her hand.

"No," he answered. "I have to go back. The Prime Minister will be expecting me. When he sent me to Lisbon he refused to let me join Wellington and the Prince Regent will already be annoyed that I have been away for so long."

Elvina knew that she had failed and once again her spirits dropped and she felt a dark wave of depression encompass her almost like the fog that they had groped their way through to Sir Rowland Hill's headquarters.

*

She was depressed for all the rest of the day. She tried to laugh and talk naturally with Lord Wye.

She tried not to count the minutes as they passed, knowing that each one brought them nearer to the time when they must board the frigate.

But relentlessly the afternoon came to an end and a hired carriage took them down the narrow streets to the quay where the frigate was berthed. Elvina had a quick glance at the ship and then turned to Lord Wye.

"You will not – forget me," she said. "Lady Cleone and her brother are your type of people, the sort you belong to. But you will not forget me – will you?"

"Elvina, what a thought!" Lord Wye exclaimed.

He turned to look at her and, as he did so often, slipped his arm around her shoulders and pulled her close.

It was a loving gesture any man might use towards a child and then he put his hand under her chin and turned her little pointed face up to his.

"Do you imagine that I could forget you even if I wanted to?" he asked. "We have been through so much together, you and me. We have faced death and starvation and even worse things, the drunken soldiers and those who would have crucified us for treachery. Do you think I could forget all that? You must have a very poor opinion of me."

The very relief that his words brought made her lips tremble and tears come into her eyes.

"It's just that – I am – afraid," she whispered.

"Afraid of what?" he asked. "The sea? Of going to England?"

"No – of losing you."

She spoke the truth because this was no time for pretence. They had reached the ship, and, although Lord Wye could not understand it, she knew that a new life lay ahead.

"You are being fanciful and absurd," he answered. "I have already promised you that you will never lose me. I think in fact that it would be hard for us to lose each other. Trust me, Elvina, I shall not fail you."

He bent his head and kissed her lips lightly. It was a kiss of tenderness and affection.

To Elvina it was as if a sudden flame flared within her body, lit by the touch of his mouth on hers. She felt herself tremble, felt her whole being quiver and only with great difficulty prevented herself from putting her arms around his neck.

"And now we must go aboard," Lord Wye said in a practical tone that swept away the emotions and the fantasies that seemed to have encompassed them both in their different ways.

The cab driver opened the door, they stepped down onto the cobbled quayside and Elvina saw ahead the gangplank leading to the frigate. She was a beautiful vessel with long clean lines and three masts.

Elvina followed Lord Wye aboard and then, even as she reached the deck, heard Lady Cleone's high affected voice.

"Your Lordship, how entrancing to see you! I swear that I have been looking forward to it the whole day."

She was curtseying, the very picture of grace and fashion, Lord Wye was bowing to her and for a second Elvina hated them both. They belonged to a world that she was an outsider in.

And then behind her she heard the Honourable Peregrine Howard's voice.

"Would you like to come and see the ship?" he asked.

She looked round at him and could not help but feel a little comforted by the friendliness of his smile and the hand he held out to her.

"Come along," he said as one might speak to a small child. "I have lots of things to show you."

He drew her away onto the bridge. He showed her the compass, the navigating wheel and the maps that were all ready for the Captain.

"We shall have to have a pilot," he told her, "to take us out of the Harbour. After that they will rely on these maps."

He was condescending, talking down to a child's intelligence and yet he was trying to be kind. But Elvina could hardly listen to him.

She was watching Lady Cleone lead Lord Wye to the side of the ship. The wind was rustling the dark curls on the front of her head as they peeped out beneath a hood of blue satin lined with swansdown.

They were talking animatedly. Lord Wye was laughing at something that Lady Cleone had said. She turned with a sudden intimate gesture and laid her hand on his arm.

'I hate her! *I hate her*!' Elvina thought.

She knew without being told that Lady Cleone was making a dead set at Lord Wye. Perhaps she had told her brother to keep that tiresome child amused while she laid her snares and set her traps for the man who had evaded matrimony for nearly thirty summers.

"You are not listening, Elvina," Peregrine Howard said accusingly.

"I am sorry. I was wondering what your sister, Lady Cleone, was saying to Lord Wye."

"Oh, don't worry about Cleone. She will be flirting," Peregrine Howard laughed. "She flirts with everyone. I had a devil of a job looking after her on this trip. I swear to you that half the garrison in Sicily was in mourning when we left!"

"Is she so attractive to men?" Elvina asked.

Peregrine Howard laughed.

"Look for yourself. She is the toast of St. James's. 'The most beautiful girl in England' the Prince Regent called her last time we went to Carlton House. And, by Jove, although she is my sister, I begin to believe he is right!"

Elvina clutched her hands together. She felt her hatred for Lady Cleone intensify. Why? Why, she wondered, had she and Lord Wye arrived in Santander yesterday instead of tomorrow?

Had they been even twenty-four hours later the frigate might have sailed without Lady Cleone becoming aware of their presence.

"Why has she not married?"

She heard her own voice ask the question and knew that instead of being hard and spiteful as she felt inside, it was young and ingenuous, the question of a child.

"I often ask myself the same question," Peregrine Howard answered good-humouredly. "I think the truth is the offers, and there have been dozens of them, have not been good enough. Cleone wants so much, as you might imagine."

"And what sort of man would you pick for her?"

"Someone with looks and breeding, position and wealth. They are few and far between, Elvina, although you would not know that, living in this unpretentious country."

Peregrine Howard was talking teasingly and telling the truth because, as Elvina sensed, he was talking as much to himself as to her.

Now she knew – knew what Lady Cleone was after and knew too that the man she had been looking for was at her side.

"*Looks and breeding, position and wealth.*"

The perfect description of Lord Wye. And she had four, or was it five, days to capture him in, days when they would be alone together he could not escape from her even if he wished to do so.

It was then that Elvina made up her mind that she would prevent it if she could.

It was not only because she loved Lord Wye herself and she knew in her heart of hearts that he could never love her and that she could never be anything in his life – but because instinctively she knew that Lady Cleone was not good enough for him.

There was no warmth of reality in her voice and there was no gentleness in her eyes.

'She is hard and she is calculating,' Elvina ruminated.

With her new resolution spurring her forward, she hurried down the companionway and crossed the deck.

She ran up to Lord Wye and slipped her arm in his.

"Come and see the maps on the bridge," she suggested. "Do come and look at them. They are not nearly as good as the ones you had on your yacht, I am convinced of it."

It was the eager interruption of a child and Lord Wye turned to smile at her.

"Are they not?" he said. "Then perhaps I shall be able to give the Captain some hints. I am rather good at drawing maps. Another accomplishment that might come in useful one day."

"You have so many," Lady Cleone said in a soft voice, her eyes looking up at him from under her long, artificially darkened lashes.

"You flatter me," Lord Wye replied. "But actually this last week I have discovered that I have unknown qualifications. For instance, I have become quite a good thief."

Lady Cleone gave a little cry.

"A thief!"

"Yes, indeed. I have learned how to get not one ration but two from the forage cart! How to purloin a piece of

Army equipment that one particularly wants from someone who has left it lying about or who is no longer in need of it. You would be astonished how expert I have become at such things."

"What you must have suffered, you poor man!" Lady Cleone burbled. "You must forget the terrible dangers that you have passed through. In fact I will do everything in my power to make you forget them."

Again that upward glance and that little pressure of a white hand on his arm.

"Come and look at the maps," Elvina insisted.

Lord Wye yielded to the pressing pull at his hand and let her lead him away from Lady Cleone on to the bridge.

"You will be interested, I know you will be," Elvina promised him.

She glanced back at Lady Cleone. She was watching them go with a tiny pout on her red lips. At the same time her eyes were assured and confident.

Elvina felt as if a hand clutched at her heart.

'She shall not have him. She shall not,' she determined. She did not, however, underrate her opponent.

That night when they sat down to dinner in the candlelit cabin a meal was served that would have done credit to any London chef.

"What delicious food!" Lord Wye exclaimed.

"You have to thank Cleone for that," her brother answered proudly. "She had a talk with the chef before we sailed and gave him some of her recipes. I assure you, sir, that in Sicily men fought to have an invitation to dinner at my father's house."

"I am not surprised," Lord Wye said.

"I have always been brought up with men," Lady Cleone came in, "and I know that, however amusing the conversation or however attractive the conversationalist, the first thing they require is to be well fed and well wined."

"I think you belie us," Lord Wye said. "Equally, as a connoisseur, I must salute you. Both the food and the wine tonight have been superlative tonight."

"I am so glad you are pleased," Lady Cleone answered and the look in her eyes made it quite obvious that she was not referring only to the food and wine.

She was looking so lovely that Elvina had to concede that in this, at any rate, there was little pretence.

She wore a gown of cherry red velvet that showed off the magnolia whiteness of her shoulders and which matched the red of her lips. There were rubies and diamonds in her ears and round her wrists. There was a long scarf of velvet lined with ermine to put around her if she went out on deck.

In the plain muslin gown made by the seamstress in Santander Elvina knew that she looked a neat, tidy and a rather unattractive child.

She had spent some time in front of the tiny looking glass in her cabin, trying to arrange her hair more appealingly. But it was quite useless.

In the end she put the little wreath of flowers and ribbons on it and hoped that Lady Cleone would not notice the fair parting and the little hint of gold on the waves that had begun to reappear now that the dye was wearing off.

'So thin, so ugly,' Elvina told herself.

Yet she knew that in her battle with Lady Cleone she had one point in her favour. Lord Wye was not on his guard against her.

She had gone to his cabin when she was ready and found him dressed except for his coat and he was tying his cravat in front of the mirror.

He too had bought some clothes in Santander, but they were quite inadequate for his needs and Peregrine Howard had put his own wardrobe at his disposal. Fortunately they were about the same height.

"Dammit!" Lord Wye exclaimed as she came into the cabin. "I have almost forgotten how to tie a cravat."

"Shall I do it for you?" Elvina asked.

"You?" he enquired. "No, you had best call Howard's valet. He said he would come to me, but I told him I could manage for myself. I thought I could. I used to be able to tie a cravat better than Wilkins."

"Was Wilkins your valet?" Elvina asked. "Well, let me take his place. I have often tied them for my father."

"Well, you can have a try," Lord Wye said in an amused voice. "If it is a failure, we will use up another of Howard's muslins."

"Sit down," Elvina suggested, pulling a chair into the centre of the cabin for him.

He did as he was told and she tied his cravat with neat, nimble little fingers.

"It may not be a fashionable style," she commented a little anxiously.

"By Jove! You have done it extremely well. Thank you, Elvina. What a wife you will make one day for a happy man!"

"I shall never get married," Elvina said quickly without thinking.

"Why not?" he asked her.

"Because I shall never want to," she replied.

"That is what you think now," Lord Wye said. "When you are older, you will find that a husband can be very convenient for a woman."

"Is a wife convenient for a man?" Elvina asked.

He shook his head.

"No, indeed. Wives are the devil. Always nagging at a fellow. I have sworn never to have one if I can help it."

"Then keep your vow," Elvina could not help saying.

"That is a betrayal of your sex," he teased her.

"Do you want to be nagged at?" she asked.

"No, indeed," he answered. "But women set traps for men and sometimes they are fool enough to fall into them."

"Not if he knows they are there."

"Who are you warning me against?" Lord Wye asked with a twinkle in his eyes. "Could it possibly be the fair Lady Cleone?"

"You must use your own judgement where she is concerned – "

"Do you not like her?" Lord Wye enquired. "I thought she was making herself extremely pleasant to you."

"Yes, indeed," Elvina replied. "She pressed a coin into the poor beggar child's hand, told her to be good and say her prayers!"

At the contempt and bitterness in Elvina's voice Lord Wye threw back his head and roared with laughter.

"You are most certainly an imp of mischief," he said. "You never miss anything do you? I thought myself that the fair Cleone was slightly patronising."

"To tell the truth I am half-afraid that she will push me overboard. You see, she has always been brought up with men."

Again Lord Wye roared with laughter.

Then he checked himself.

"Elvina, we are being disloyal and rather discourteous," he said severely. "Lady Cleone has most kindly offered us hospitality. We must not abuse it."

"No, indeed, I am sorry," Elvina replied in pretended embarrassment.

But she knew that her little shafts had gone home and Lord Wye would remember them. What was more, he would be warned.

When dinner was over, Lady Cleone drew Lord Wye onto a comfortable sofa and talked to him in a soft voice, asking him to tell of his experiences on the outward voyage, begging him to tell stories of the Prince Regent and altogether flattering him into talking about himself.

Peregrine Howard made an effort to entertain Elvina. She answered him only in monosyllables, sitting watching Lady Cleone and Lord Wye until she said a little irritably,

"I think it's time for little girls went to bed, do not you?"

As if suddenly awakened to his responsibilities. Lord Wye said quickly,

"Yes, Elvina, you must be tired."

"I am not in the least tired"

"But indeed you are, although you may not know it," Lady Cleone said. "This past week must have taken a toll of your health and strength and we must take care of you on this voyage, must we not, my Lord?"

"We surely must," he said a little hastily. "Go to bed, Elvina. Try and sleep late."

Elvina would have protested, but she felt that to do so would have made her merely seem difficult and that, above all things, she did not wish to appear.

She rose to her feet, made a curtsey to Lady Cleone and then bent forward and kissed Lord Wye on the cheek.

She felt herself blush as she did so for he put his arm around her, pulled her close to him and kissed her in return, a warm loving kiss that made her very skin tingle.

"Have a good night," he said. "We have to fatten you up before we reach England."

"Thank you, but I would rather remain just as I am," Elvina said untruthfully.

She turned away, curtseying to Peregrine Howard and left the Saloon.

Before the door had closed behind her she heard Lady Cleone say,

"Poor little thing. We must try and help her and perhaps, if she is fatter, she will not be so excessively plain."

Elvina shut the door and stood for a moment shaking with rage.

She wanted to go back and confront Lady Cleone, to tell her that she would be plain if she had lived the life that she had, beaten and undernourished, treated like a servant by her stepmother and run off her feet with the amount of work there was to do and for which the only thanks she had were blows and slaps.

And then she realised that to make a scene would only make her appear vulgar and ill-bred. Lady Cleone had it all her own way.

She was lovely and had a background which, although they had never met, she shared with Lord Wye because they belonged to the same stratum of Society.

She had managed at dinner to talk of friends and acquaintances in a manner that made their conversation intimate and Elvina and Peregrine Howard might not have existed.

There was no possible opening for them when they could join in the conversation.

Elvina's cabin was next door, but she did not go to it. She walked slowly across the deck.

The sea was calm, but there was a fair evening breeze and they were moving at a good speed.

In the West the last glimmer of the sun was going down over the sea and above the stars were coming out and twinkling in the clear sky.

Elvina leaned over the side of the ship. It was hard to believe that only a few days ago the sea had been tempestuous and cruel.

She wondered, if they had travelled straight to England on Lord Wye's yacht, whether she would have fallen in love with him, whether he would ever have meant so much to her had he remained just the elegant dandy, the gentleman who had befriended her and had not, because of the dangers they had been in together, become a companion, a protector and a friend.

'I love him!' she told the sea.

'I love him!' she told the setting sun.

'I love him!' she told the stars.

How long she stood there she did not know. She only knew that her love for Lord Wye seemed indelibly linked with all the beauty around her.

The sun went down, the twilight turned to darkness and then suddenly she heard a step behind her and turned to see Lord Wye standing there alone.

"Elvina, why are you not in bed?"

She had no answer for that question. It seemed so long ago since she left the cabin. She was suffused with her love of him and it was hard to remember that he was real and not just the embodiment of her dreams and yearnings.

She must have shivered for he put his arm around her.

"You are cold," he remarked. "It was naughty of you not to go to bed."

"I-I wanted to – think," she managed to stammer.

"And what were you thinking about?" he asked.

"Of you," she replied.

He bent down suddenly and picked her up in his arms.

"Silly little imp. Are you really regretting the nights we spent on the mountains with the troops?"

"We were – happy," Elvina murmured.

"I never realised until now how happy we were," he answered. "Strange how one looks back and finds that one felt something so much different from what one expected. We were happy, Elvina, but why are we talking as if everything is in the past. There is the future ahead of us and lots more happiness."

She did not answer him. She was just content that he was holding her in his arms with her head against his shoulder and her face so close to his as it had been when he carried her through the fog on the mountain.

"Silly child," he said with a sudden gentleness and, bending his head, kissed her forehead.

"You are half-asleep," he went on. "I am going to carry you to bed."

The ship gave a little lurch and his arms tightened about her.

"Come along," he urged. "Sentimentalising over the past is going to get us nowhere."

He carried her across the deck and bending his head managed, by pushing open the door with his shoulder, to carry her into her cabin.

He set her down gently on the bunk and he would have released her, but she put up her arms suddenly and held him close.

"Don't go," she said.

She did not quite know what she meant. She only knew that she wanted him to stay, she could not bear him to leave her.

He gave her a little hug and then released her clinging hands, stroking her hair back from her forehead.

"You are sleepy and so am I, Elvina. Goodnight, little one, and stop regretting the past. There are wonderful things to do together in the future."

He went from the cabin closing the door behind him. When he had gone Elvina let the tears roll slowly down her cheeks.

"Wonderful things to do together in the future!"

She repeated the words over and over again, crying from sheer happiness because he had uttered the one word that mattered – *together*!

CHAPTER NINE

"We shall be on English soil this afternoon," a voice came from behind Elvina.

She turned swiftly. The Honourable Peregrine Howard was standing beside her, a telescope to his eye.

She felt her heart sink. For the last four days she had enjoyed the voyage more than she could ever explain in words.

It had been rough.

Not rough enough to be dangerous or to inconvenience herself or Lord Wye in any way, but it had kept Lady Cleone in her cabin and it had made her brother spend his time with his feet up and a brandy bottle beside him.

It was wonderful for Elvina to have Lord Wye to herself, to be with him and to talk to him, to laugh and even argue without danger, without discomfort and without feeling that every word and every look might betray them.

The good food aboard the frigate, combined with the rest and, in Lady Cleone's absence, peace of mind, had made Elvina feel quite different.

She was no longer tense and nervous. She no longer slept restlessly, waking as she had the first nighty at every creak of the moving vessel.

But now her happiness was to end and her eyes were troubled as she answered Peregrine Howard.

"So soon? I thought we would not reach Harbour until evening."

"You underestimate the speed we are travelling at," he answered. "Personally, I shall be glad to step ashore. I have long thought the sea a dead bore, especially when it makes me feel indisposed."

He was a bad colour, she thought critically, and there were heavy pouches under his eyes from the excessive drinking that he had been indulging in.

"Before we go ashore I want to talk to you," he went on before she could speak.

"To me?" Elvina asked in surprise.

She wondered why she had ever thought that the Honourable Peregrine Howard was nice. She supposed that in contrast to Lady Cleone he had at first seemed pleasant and even kind.

Now she noticed that for all his good looks there was a meanness about his rather tight mouth and a hardness in his eyes that made her wonder if he would ever do an entirely disinterested act of kindness.

"Yes, to you," he answered a little heavily. "I have been talking to my sister about you."

Elvina stiffened.

"I do not wish Lady Cleone to trouble herself on my behalf," she pointed out.

"Ah. But she *is* troubled!" Peregrine Howard replied. "She is wondering what will become of you when we reach England. After all you cannot expect Lord Wye to inconvenience himself to any large extent. He is a very important personage and a child of your age could be nothing but an encumbrance."

"You need not concern yourselves on my account," Elvina replied in a low voice. "I will try not to be a nuisance – to his Lordship."

"That is what I hoped you would say," Peregrine Howard remarked approvingly. "In fact Cleone was certain that you would see sense, so she suggests, with great generosity I may say, that she will herself find you a place in a school which she is charitably interested in.

"It is an excellent place, a Seminary in fact for the daughters of reduced gentlefolk and you will be taught so that when you grow a little older you will be qualified to act as a Governess in some decent household or to occupy any other position consistent with your station."

Elvina's hands on the rail around the deck tightened until the knuckles showed white.

"I am very sensible of Lady Cleone's kindness," she said in a low voice, "but neither you nor her Ladyship could have realised that I am travelling to England – to find my sister. Lord Wye knows of this. It is the reason why he allowed me to accompany him in the first place."

She knew without looking at him that Peregrine Howard's face cleared.

"Oh, in that case there will be no need for my sister to trouble herself!" he exclaimed and his voice was light.

"Please convey my gratitude – to Lady Cleone," Elvina said.

Peregrine Howard cleared his throat.

"I think I will go and tell her right away," he smiled. "She will be pleased to hear the good news."

He moved away and Elvina, looking after him, felt herself tremble with rage and indignation and then forced herself to give a little uncertain laugh.

Lady Cleone must be frightened of her, she thought, if she was in such a hurry to dispose of her. It was obvious that she would do anything to entice her away from Lord Wye's side.

Peregrine Howard must have carried tales of how they had laughed at luncheon and dinner, how Lord Wye had seemed amused by her and how he would often caress her hair or put his arm around her shoulders to draw her close to him.

Peregrine Howard had been feeling so ill the last few days that he had not contributed much to the conversation.

But Elvina had learned, more by intuition than by anything said in words, that he and his sister were not as rich as they appeared.

Elvina suspected, and rightly so, that Lady Cleone had gone out to Sicily to visit her father in the hope of finding some aristocratic young Officer under his command who would be beguiled into offering her his hand and his heart.

Unfortunately, as only Lady Cleone and Peregrine knew, the only offers she had were one from an impecunious Subaltern, on whose part it was sheer impudence, and another from Lord Severn's second-in-command that, to put it bluntly, did not include marriage.

Standing alone, looking out to where the outline of the English coast was already faintly visible on the horizon, Elvina felt a sudden fear of what lay ahead.

These last four days seemed, in retrospect, almost to have been very near to her idea of Heaven.

Never before had anyone sought her opinion, laughed at her jokes and told her in so many words that she was adorable. Granted all that she received from Lord Wye was the affection of a grown man for a child. But for the moment that was enough to content her.

She loved him! She loved him so much that every moment when he was not near was an agony of apprehension lest he should not return.

She loved him so that when he was there she was content just with his very nearness.

She asked for nothing more than that this voyage should go on forever.

She went to sleep thinking of him, knowing that in the morning she would rise as soon as she awoke so as to hurry on the moment when he would come on deck and his face would light up at the sight of her.

"Good morning, little one!" he would say. "I thought I would be here before you."

He taught her to play piquet and they indulged in long-drawn-out battles together when if Elvina won she would clap her hands with delight and Lord Wye would declare it was unfair that the pupil should beat the teacher.

Once or twice they had arguments on serious subjects, but usually Lord Wye was the instructor and Elvina listened wide-eyed and utterly happy because she could hold his attention.

Now all that was to come to an end.

She thought of the mythical sister who had proved so useful for her story, first to Lord Wye and now to prevent Lady Cleone striving in so-called charity to put her in a Seminary.

"How dare she?" Elvina whispered to herself. "How dare she think of such a thing?"

And yet she knew that even Lord Wye might think it a kindly action on Lady Cleone's part.

'Whatever happens I must not get into her clutches,' Elvina thought.

It seemed to her as if the sunshine had suddenly gone from the day and everything was grey and rather cold.

"Why are you looking so serious, little one?"

She heard Lord Wye coming across the deck, but she had not turned as usual to greet him because she was afraid that he would see the trouble in her eyes and question her.

"I was feeling – sad," she answered quickly, "because this voyage must come – to an end."

"You have enjoyed it so much?" he asked.

She turned then and saw how well he was looking and so smart in the blue coat of Peregrine Howard's, which became him so well, the white cravat round his neck and tight breeches ending in black hessian boots that were polished until she could see the reflection of her own gown in them.

"I have loved – every moment of it," she said in a low voice.

His grey eyes were tender as he smiled at her and at the sudden passion in her voice.

"I had no idea you were such a good sailor. I can see that I shall have to buy myself another yacht."

She felt her heart leap at the implication of his words and then, gazing at the coastline growing nearer, Lord Wye said,

"I must travel at all possible speed to London. Heaven knows what the Prince Regent and the Prime Minister will imagine has happened to me. Will you come with me or will you travel more comfortably with Lady Cleone and her brother?"

"I must come with you. Please – take me."

"It will not be a very pleasant journey," Lord Wye cautioned.

"It will be pleasant enough if I can be with you. Promise me – please promise me, that you will not leave me behind."

The anxiety in her little face touched him.

"Of course, if you wish to come," he answered lightly. "But Cleone will think it is too much for you."

"Do you believe that after all we have been through?" Elvina asked. "Did I go sick on that – long march? Did I complain? What does Lady Cleone know of – hunger and discomfort?"

There was such scorn in her voice that Lord Wye said rapidly,

"Now, now, Elvina! Lady Cleone was but thinking of you. After all you are but a child."

"I am coming with you. You promised me and nothing shall – stop me," Elvina asserted.

"As you wish," Lord Wye said. "But I warn you, we have to travel fast."

It could not be too fast, Elvina thought, to get away from Lady Cleone, but she did not say it aloud and she did not have a chance to say much more for at that moment Lady Cleone came on deck.

She was looking exquisite, even her worst enemy would have to concede her that. She was rather pale and the seasickness that she had suffered from had made her a little thinner, sharpening her beauty.

She was dressed in a travelling gown of soft blue bombazine with a bonnet trimmed with the same coloured feathers and a stole draped over her shoulders. Holding onto her brother's arm, she was the very picture of fragile but alluring womanhood.

When she saw Lord Wye, she moved swiftly towards him, both hands outstretched.

"My Lord!" she exclaimed, her eyes raised to his imploringly. "How can I ever ask you to forgive me? I am so ashamed and so utterly humiliated, that I had to desert you. It was so miserable for me, yet what could I do? I was prostrate, utterly prostrate, until this morning. And now I can only crave your understanding."

She looked so pretty making her apologies that it would take a heart of steel to resist her.

"My dear Lady Cleone," Lord Wye answered, "there is nothing to forgive. We were only desolate at your absence, utterly and completely desolate."

'It's not true!' Elvina longed to cry.

Instead she could only watch Lady Cleone press Lord Wye's hands and murmur,

"You are too kind. If you only knew how angry I have been with myself."

Lord Wye raised her hand to his lips.

"You are better now, which is all that matters."

Lady Cleone turned to Elvina.

"And how are you, child?" she asked. "My brother has told me that you have been in good health. I only hope that you will not feel the reaction later."

"I am very well," Elvina answered, dropping a polite curtsey.

"Well, we will take great care of you," Lady Cleone said. "You shall drive with me to London and we will not make the journey too arduous."

"I am going with Lord Wye," Elvina said quickly.

Lady Cleone raised her eyebrows.

"I do not think that would be at all a good idea," she answered softly. "His Lordship will be in a hurry and will not wish to be held back by feminine frailty."

She gave a little sigh.

"You will find, dear, that we women must often stand aside and let the strong male go his way alone."

Elvina moved swiftly to Lord Wye's side.

"You promised," she said earnestly. "You *promised*."

"Yes, that is true," Lord Wye answered. "I am afraid, Lady Cleone, I have promised Elvina that she can come with me. She is used to hardship and will not find the speed that I have to reach London in too exhausting."

Lady Cleone's eyes were veiled as she responded,

"It must, of course, be as your Lordship wishes. I would have been glad of Elvina's company as I feel a little weak and might be inclined to faint."

Lord Wye hesitated and Elvina knew that this was an appeal that was far more likely to succeed than any that Lady Cleone had produced so far.

"I think her Ladyship would be wise to rest for a few days," she said quickly. "If she went to the hotel, she would then have time to engage a maidservant and one would, I am sure, be far more useful than – I could ever be."

"That is indeed a good idea," Lord Wye said. "Your Ladyship must allow me to engage you rooms at *The Saracen's Head* which, if I remember rightly, is the best hotel in Southampton."

"Peregrine can do all that is necessary," Lady Cleone replied and there was a sudden sharpness in her voice that Elvina did not miss.

There was also a glint of steel in her Ladyship's liquid eyes as she looked at Elvina for one brief second before she placed her hand once more on her brother's arm.

"I should like to sit down in the sunshine," she said.

The gentlemen hovered around her, fetching a rug for her knees and a cushion for her back. She had lost the first round of her match with Elvina, but that did not say she would not win the next.

In fact before they arrived in Southampton, Lady Cleone had Lord Wye not only dancing attendance on her but arranging that they should meet the very moment she and her brother arrived in London.

"I have always been consumed with a passion to see the inside of Wye House," Lady Cleone confessed. "My father and yours were, as you know, great friends and Papa has often spoken of your paintings. 'One of the finest collections in England' was how he described them."

"I am most fortunate in the possessions I inherited," Lord Wye answered. "But most of my pictures have been moved from London to my country seat, Combe Park, in Hertfordshire."

"And dare I hope for an invitation to see them there?" Lady Cleone asked.

"The invitation is already at your feet. Combe Park invites you to visit as soon as it can possibly be arranged."

"How kind you are," Lady Cleone said. "For this time of the year I find London unbearably stuffy. I imagine that the Prince Regent himself will soon be going to Brighthelmstone."

"He may be there now for all I know," Lord Wye stated.

"Well, we must meet in London and make plans," Lady Cleone suggested. "I will send a note to Wye House as soon as Peregrine and I arrive. We shall be staying with my aunt, Lady D'Arcy. Her house is not very comfortable and I assure you that the thought of a visit to Combe Park will fill my dreams with happy anticipation."

'She is clever,' Elvina ruminated. 'How very clever she is!'

With a little sinking of her heart she wondered how she could ever think for a moment of competing with anyone so experienced and so subtle as Lady Cleone.

At last they managed to say 'goodbye'. It all took a great deal of time, to steer the frigate into the Harbour, to pass the Customs Officers and then go ashore.

Elvina more than once thought desperately that even Lord Wye would not be able to hasten things and they would be left to spend the night in Southampton with Lady Cleone.

Then, by some magic of his own and an authority that he seemed to exert so effortlessly and yet so autocratically that people flew to do his bidding, a curricle drawn by two fast horses appeared and, having lifted Elvina up beside him, Lord Wye took the reins himself.

There was a groom to sit behind, his arms folded, his top hat pulled firmly down over his ears as if he anticipated that they would be travelling fast and then they had moved away while Lady Cleone was still standing on the quayside, her luggage being carried to the shore by sailors.

Elvina saw her face as they drove away and almost laughed aloud. And then, almost immediately, she knew that in reality she had nothing to laugh about.

There was a determination in Lady Cleone's tightly shut lips and there was something forceful in the set of her little chin that boded ill for the future.

The horses were fresh and Lord Wye let them have their heads. The afternoon was hot and sultry and it was a relief to feel the cool air on her cheeks, Elvina thought.

She had been lamentably conscious as they came ashore of how dowdy she looked beside the elegance of Lady Cleone. Her gown, made by the Portuguese seamstress, was, as she had anticipated at the time, pathetically out of fashion.

Her bonnet looked cheap and humble beside Lady Cleone's concoction of ribbon, lace and feathers.

For a moment Elvina had felt like crying out,

'Leave me behind! I am too shabby to come with you.'

And then, as they drove away, she was conscious of an absolute passion of gratitude towards the man at her side. She was not concerned with her looks.

He liked her just as she was and she could never thank him enough in her heart for giving her a confidence that she was sadly lacking in.

"This is surprisingly good horseflesh," Lord Wye was remarking. "But wait until you see my greys. If we had them with us now, we would do the journey in half the time."

He was silent for a moment as they came to a rather difficult turning and then he went on,

"I will have to teach you to hold the ribbons. It is not really a ladylike accomplishment, but you are young enough for it not to matter what people think."

"I have never worried about them," Elvina said quickly.

"Some women think of nothing else," Lord Wye said and then he added, "But I had forgotten, you will be wanting to go to your sister, will you not?"

"I have to – find her first."

"Oh, that should not be difficult," Lord Wye replied. "What did you say was the name of your brother-in-law?"

"Thompson," Elvina answered. "Robert Thompson."

"And his Regiment?"

There was a little pause.

"It is – so silly of me," Elvina stammered, "but for the moment I cannot remember it. It may have been the – Light Dragoons, but then again it might have been the – Hussars. There have been so many Regiments in Lisbon, I just cannot remember."

"Try and describe his uniform," Lord Wye suggested.

"He wore a r-red coat," Elvina said hastily.

"Hmm! Sounds as if we have not much to go on, but I will get someone to make enquiries at the War Office. They keep the Army Lists there."

"Thank you," Elvina said in a low voice.

"Until then you can stay at Wye House or come down to Combe Park. You will like my country seat. It is very beautiful."

"I was already thinking that the country in England is so lovely," Elvina sighed, looking around her as they drove through a narrow lane, the hedgerows covered with honeysuckle and the verges ablaze with wild flowers.

"To me there is nowhere as glorious as England," Lord Wye said quietly.

Then he added,

"But, of course, you feel the same about your own country."

Elvina longed to tell him that England was her own country too, but she was afraid to say too much. She wondered how long she must keep up the pretence and then knew that she dared not risk what she already had, because to lose it would leave her utterly bereft of everything that mattered to her.

They drove on until it was very late and stopped for dinner at a country inn, changed horses and drove on again until it was dark.

Elvina would not have complained for the world, but she was tired when finally she was shown up the oak stairs of a small inn by a fat landlady and ushered into a bedchamber that smelt of lavender and contained a large bed with a feather mattress.

Elvina had meant to lie awake thinking over the events of the day and of what she had said to Lord Wye and what he had said to her.

But the moment her head touched the pillow she fell asleep and awoke only when the curtains were being drawn back and the landlady was placing a cup of chocolate beside her bed.

*

"It is morning?" she asked in a sleepy voice, still hardly roused from her dreams.

"Only just," the landlady said with a chuckle. "'Tis six of the clock and 'is Lordship be that impatient to be gone you'd think the Runners were at 'is 'eels. Breakfast will be on the table in a quarter of an hour."

The mere words 'his Lordship' woke Elvina more effectively than anything else.

She flew out of bed, washed herself in cold water, slipped into her clothes, drank the chocolate and was downstairs just as the big dishes of eggs and bacon were being carried in piping hot from the kitchen.

"Are you tired?" Lord Wye asked her. "I warned you that you would not have much rest."

"I feel ready for anything," Elvina retorted.

It was true, for at the mere sight of him she felt as if champagne had been poured into her veins.

They had another day together!

Another day alone, another day when he could talk to her and tell her all the things she wanted to hear.

"I am not being a nuisance – am I?" she asked. "You see, I am down as early as you are."

"You are never a nuisance," he replied. "And it is fun to have you with me. I want to show you some of the sights as we near London. I might even take you to Vauxhall Gardens this week if the Prince Regent does not want me."

"Oh, would you? I should love that above – all things."

"You are such a child. It will be amusing to show you the places that I enjoyed when I was a boy, the aquarium, for instance. That was one of my favourite spots."

"What about – Lady Cleone?"

Elvina could not help the question. The mere thought of Lady Cleone was like some dark snake within the Eden of her happiness.

"Oh, I had not forgotten her," Lord Wye answered. "I must give a dinner party as soon as she arrives in London. She is very beautiful, Elvina. I am rather surprised that I have not met her before."

"Yes, she is – beautiful," Elvina responded in a quiet voice.

She left the rest of her breakfast, she was no longer hungry.

That day Lord Wye pushed the horses even harder.

They changed three times and he gave himself nor Elvina any rest save that they ate while fresh horses were being put between the shafts and they were ready to move on almost before the grooms had finished fastening the harnesses.

Elvina was so tired when night came that she could scarcely keep her eyes open.

"Have a glass of wine," Lord Wye suggested.

She drank a glass of claret, but it made her sleepier still. The inn they were staying at was bigger and more comfortable than the one where they had stayed the night before and Lord Wye had ordered a heavy dinner.

He himself was hungry and he was not particularly tired. In fact the drive was exhilarating to him because he always liked to be doing something.

There was nothing he found more tedious than sitting about, as Peregrine Howard and his cronies liked to do, playing a game of cards for high stakes and spending the rest of the day drinking.

"You know, Elvina," he said, as he helped himself to another slice of boiled mutton, "one ought to spend more time touring England. Everyone has complained that they cannot do the Grand Tour of Europe because of the War. Why not visit one's own country? Shall we start a new fashion, you and I, driving North to Yorkshire and Northumberland and driving South to Devon and Cornwall?"

"That would be lovely," Elvina agreed.

She wanted to say how wonderful it would be to drive with him anywhere, to Hell itself if necessary, but the words would not come between her lips.

She had put down her knife and fork some time ago although the food on her plate was not half-consumed. And now she leaned back against her chair and her head fell against the winged sides and stayed there.

"I will tell you what we will do," Lord Wye began and then he looked up.

Elvina was asleep, fast asleep, and his eyes softened at the sight of her.

Poor child! It had been a hard day and yet she had never complained. Cleone had been right. He expected too much.

She should have gone to London in a more leisurely manner rather than racketing along beside him.

Then he remembered the urgency and the appeal in her voice.

"You promised! *You promised!*"

He could hear her saying it and knew that if he had forced her to go with Cleone it might have well nigh broken her heart.

'Oh, well,' he told himself, 'we are nearly there and we will not have such a long day tomorrow.'

He finished his meal and told the landlord to bring another bottle of wine.

"What about the young lady?" the landlord asked. "Will she be wantin' anythin'?"

"I think all she wants is her bed," Lord Wye smiled.

"I'll fetch the missus," the landlord suggested, "and I'll carry her up. No need to wake her."

"When your wife is ready, I will carry her up myself," Lord Wye replied.

"Very good, my Lord."

A few minutes later there came a knock at the door.

The innkeeper's wife came into the sitting room holding a lighted candle.

"I have prepared a bed, my Lord," she said, dropping a curtsey. "If you will carry the young lady upstairs, I will get her undressed without wakin' her. My husband was tellin' me you've come a long way today."

"A long way indeed and it has been hot."

"That it has," the innkeeper's wife agreed. "'Tis the heat that takes it out of you. That's what the harvesters were sayin'."

She was talking all the time that she led the way upstairs, but Lord Wye was not listening. He was thinking how small and light Elvina was in his arms. Only a child and yet she had the heart and courage of a lion.

He would look after her, he thought, if she did not find her sister and, if she did, he would see that she was comfortably provided for. He owed her so much.

It was a debt that money could never wipe out.

He set her down gently on the bed. Elvina stirred, but she did not wake up. He bent over her and heard her murmur in her sleep.

"I love – him!" she was saying, almost beneath her breath.

Lord Wye stood looking down at her.

There was an expression of tenderness on his face that made the innkeeper's wife wipe her eyes.

CHAPTER TEN

The day had started badly.

When Elvina came down to breakfast in the oak-beamed sitting room of the inn, it was to find the landlord regaling Lord Wye with a long description of the groom's sickness during the night.

"Maybe it were summat 'e 'ad eaten, my Lord," the landlord said. "But it were not what 'e 'ad in this 'ouse. Comin' as late as you did, 'e ate almost the same as your Lordship and you've 'ad a good night, I can tell it by the look of you."

"I slept well," Lord Wye replied. "But I am sorry to learn that my groom is indisposed. Is he too ill to travel?"

"That 'e be," the innkeeper replied. "Lyin' in the straw above the 'orses, claspin' 'is stomach and groanin' so you can 'ear 'im right across the yard."

"I will speak to him when I have had my breakfast," Lord Wye said.

"Very good, my Lord."

The landlord hurried away to come back with the inevitable dish of eggs and bacon, a great ham, which he assured them was from a prize porker bred in the village, and a brawn that he boasted was made from the finest recipe in the whole county of Surrey.

"What will you do if the groom is too ill to travel?" Elvina asked when they were alone.

"Send for the local physician and leave him enough money to make his own way back to Southampton," Lord Wye replied. "We shall not need him. We shall be in London this afternoon."

Elvina heard this with a sense of dismay.

Although she had known that the journey must end some time, she had snatched at these days alone with Lord Wye, feeling that each one of them was full of enchantment and every hour with him was precious.

"Is London – very big?" she asked with a little tremble in her voice.

"It depends on how you view it," Lord Wye replied. "For those who are socially inclined it is a small circle of those you know. The ones outside that circle are not of the least consequence."

"My mother always said one should know people of every world and – every class of Society," Elvina said.

She spoke without thinking and then saw Lord Wye look at her closely.

"This is the first time you have mentioned your mother. What was she like?"

"Very lovely," Elvina answered almost defiantly.

"That I can believe. Was she of some noble family in Portugal?"

Elvina felt her face burn and she dropped her head a little lower.

"I – think so," she mumbled.

How she hated to lie to Lord Wye and yet the moment had not come when she could tell him the truth. Besides, she had plans in her mind, plans only half-formed, but nevertheless there.

She could not speak of them until she had seen London and until she knew what lay ahead of her.

It was a warm sunny morning with the promise of great heat later in the afternoon. The new horses provided at the inn were an excellent pair used to running together and they set off at a spanking pace.

Elvina felt a sudden rush of happiness. She longed to put her hand on Lord Wye's knee to tell him how happy she was.

And yet, because she loved him so deeply, it was far more difficult for her to express herself than had she been the child that he believed her to be.

The roads were now good, far better than the lanes they had encountered when they first left Southampton.

There was very little traffic and although they occasionally met a stagecoach or a closed carriage with a Nobleman's arms painted on the panel, the other travellers were mostly driving hay carts and moving very slowly from one part of the farm to the other.

"This is very different from the Dover road," Lord Wye remarked, "and when the Prince Regent is repairing to Brighthelmstone, one can barely move above a snail's pace for the congestion of carriages, coaches, phaetons and curricles."

They had luncheon at a charming little country inn and, having changed horses, set off again. Elvina had never known Lord Wye so gay and animated and she thought with a little stab of the heart that it was because he was nearing London.

Lord Wye seemed not to notice that she answered him only in monosyllables, her spirits sinking lower and lower, the heat of the sun and the misery in her own mind seeming to stifle everything she would have said in response to all that he was telling her.

"As soon as we reach London, I must report to the Prime Minister exactly what happened during our sojourn with the French forces," Lord Wye was saying. "He has often said to me that he thought that Bonaparte was running short of men. When he learns about that last pitiable Division which arrived from Paris when we were in St. Jean de Luz, it will confirm his most optimistic hopes. Boys of sixteen, emaciated, overgrown and without the stamina to stand up to Wellington's seasoned troops. Poor little devils! I have it in my heart to be sorry for them."

"Yes," Elvina replied.

Seeing in her mind's eye not the white-faced, exhausted French boys crowded round the food carts, but Lord Wye sheltering her from the drunken roistering troops. Lord Wye pulling her up the hill by the hand. Lord Wye holding her close beside him as they lay in the open on the rough mountainside.

They were now passing through a wooded part of the country, the road rising to the top of the hill and twisting a little through high beech trees.

It was then, unexpectedly, without any warning, that a horseman suddenly galloped from the shadow of the trees across their path.

"Stand and deliver!"

The words were shouted out in a coarse ugly tone and Lord Wye pulled the horses to a standstill, the curricle shaking as they plunged against the tightness of the reins.

"What the devil!" Elvina heard him exclaim and then there was another man at their side also on horseback, his face half-covered by a black mask and an ugly-looking pistol held in his hand pointing straight at Lord Wye's heart.

"Get down and give us your valuables," he demanded roughly.

"Why should I do that?" Lord Wye enquired.

"Unless you want a bullet in your gullet, you'll do as you're told," was the answer.

Elvina gave a little cry. She recognised the threat for what it was and knew that men such as those who faced them now would not stick at murder.

"Please," she murmured, "please – do as they say."

Lord Wye glanced down at her.

"You are frightening the lady I have with me," he said.

"If she knows what is good for 'er she'll give us any sparklers she may 'ave on her," the highwayman said. "Hurry now! We 'aven't time to stand about all day."

The man who had stopped the horses had now dismounted and gone to their heads. Elvina noticed with relief that he slipped his pistol into his belt so as to leave his hands free.

His own horse, obviously used to such diversions, moved leisurely to one side and started cropping the grass.

Slowly, almost maddeningly slowly, Elvina thought in her fear, Lord Wye got down into the road and stood for a moment, hesitant, his eyes roaming towards the small portmanteau he carried in the back of the curricle.

There was not much in it, as Elvina knew only too well, only a few clean shirts and cravats that Peregrine Howard had lent him for the journey. The trunk was his also.

To her astonishment Lord Wye said, in what appeared a most unconvincing manner,

"There is nothing, nothing, I assure you, in my baggage."

"We'll soon see about that," the highwayman said, obviously suspicious. "Open it up."

With an obvious reluctance Lord Wye drew off his driving gloves and started fumbling at the straps of the portmanteau.

He was being so clumsy at getting them undone that Elvina almost offered to help him because she was so anxious to escape from the situation that they now found themselves in.

"Hurry! Hurry!" the highwayman said angrily, digging the point of his pistol into Lord Wye's ribs.

He stood beside him.

"I cannot get them undone," Lord Wye said. "My fingers are stiff. Besides, as I have told you, there is nothing in them that could possibly interest you."

"I'm the best judge of that," the highwayman answered. "'Ere, Jed, come and give the cove an 'and. The 'orses are quiet enough."

"There is nothing there," Lord Wye expostulated. "Nothing. Let me give you my purse."

He turned as if to pull the purse from his trousers pocket.

"Get that portmanteau open," the highwayman almost shouted. "That's where the gold is. Come on, Jed."

They both put out a hand towards the stiff leather straps and as they did so Lord Wye acted.

He caught the first highwayman, who had been concerned with the horses, a tremendous blow in the stomach.

The other man turned to fire at him but he knocked the pistol up and it exploded harmlessly into the air.

Then he caught the man a crashing blow under the chin that seemed to lift him right into the air before he collapsed on his back in the road.

The other man was doubled up with the pain of the blow.

Lord Wye hit him again, knocking him sideways onto the grass verge and then, almost before Elvina could draw her breath, he had sprung into the curricle, picked up the reins and they were moving off.

The report from the pistol was still ringing in her ears. She felt the horses move forward in obedience to the whip and, with a little gasp of astonishment and relief, realised that they were free.

She looked back. The highwaymen were still. One in the centre of the road, the other on the side. Neither was moving, while their horses unconcernedly cropped the grass.

"Oh, you were – wonderful! *Wonderful!*" she breathed. "I was so frightened, so afraid they would – shoot you."

"Not a pleasant situation," Lord Wye muttered, "not with you beside me."

"I was so – frightened," Elvina said again.

She only realised now just how terrified she had been. The paralysis that seemed to have gripped her the moment the highwayman had called out 'stand and deliver' ebbed away and she felt her heart beating and her body trembling with fear of what might have been.

"They – m-might have – killed you," she said, her voice shaking with the horror of it.

"Surely by now you know that I do not die easily," Lord Wye answered.

His eyes were twinkling and his mouth was smiling. He was elated by what had happened. It was the sort of adventure he enjoyed.

"If they had – killed you, I should have – wanted to die too," Elvina faltered.

He laughed at the tragedy in her tones and, taking one hand from the reins, he put it round her shoulders and drew her close to him.

"It's all over," he said reassuringly.

"You were – splendid!"

She hardly breathed the words above a whisper, but her lips were parted and her eyes shining like stars. He looked down and instinctively bent his head to kiss her.

He had meant to touch her cheek as he had done so often before, but somehow his lips met hers and her mouth clung to his.

The kiss she gave him was not the kiss of a child, it was the kiss of a woman who loves and whose every nerve tingles at the touch of the man she adores.

Just for a moment his lips remained on hers and then he jerked up his head, his face drained of all colour beneath his tan.

Elvina felt him draw a deep breath.

Then his hand, which had been round her shoulders, went up to his forehead to wipe away the sudden beads of sweat on his brow.

"I must be crazed!" she heard him say almost beneath his breath.

Then they were driving on in silence, both of them looking straight ahead, both of them tinglingly aware that something momentous had happened.

It was Elvina who was the most dismayed.

She realised that she had betrayed herself and yet she knew that Lord Wye did not understand and was in fact amazed and horrified at the feelings that she had aroused in him.

She could still feel the touch of his lips on her mouth.

The kiss seemed to burn itself through her whole body making her feel as if she was on fire with a sudden wonder and happiness that she had never know before.

They drove on to London almost in silence until, just as the sun was sinking, they became one with the coaches and drays all travelling towards the centre of the City.

For a moment Elvina forgot her feelings, her problems and even the difficulties that lay ahead as she gazed at the shops with their glistening panes and smart bow windows, huddled against lowly dwellings through whose open doors she could see cobblers and artisans at work.

There were coal wagons and blaspheming draymen. There were street organs and musicians playing tambourines and fiddles. There were boys and men shouting that they had hot and cold food for sale.

There were crowds of beggars holding out their hands to foot passengers so elegantly and richly dressed that Elvina could only stare at them in astonishment.

She had not expected the outward appearance of London to be so prosperous. She had not thought to see, not one carriage with gilded, painted doors, the horses sparkling with silver harness, but dozens in every street that they passed through.

She had not imagined hundreds of huge tall houses with porticoed doors and a labyrinth of streets that seemed to her very wide after the cobbled lanes of Lisbon.

There were herds of cattle too being driven out of the City after they had come in that morning to bring their milk for those who needed it. They were fat animals with glossy coats, apparently quite unperturbed or frightened by the milling throngs around them.

There were women selling lavender and flowers and vegetables, but even they seemed to Elvina to be far better dressed than she had ever been and their fair hair and clear rosy complexions made her long to dispense with her own darkened skin and be as she had looked before she disguised herself.

"We have not far to go now," Lord Wye remarked. "Are you tired?"

She thought the restraint had gone from his voice and she answered with deliberate childishness.

"I am not tired because it's – so exciting. What a lot of people live in London!"

"Too many. It takes a man nearly an hour to get to the country now and when I was a boy it was little more than ten minutes."

The horses were tired, but they seemed to realise that they were nearing comfortable stables for they managed to make good speed up Piccadilly.

Lord Wye turned them expertly down Berkeley Street and on reaching Berkeley Square they drew up in front of what seemed to Elvina a palatial house with double doors, each surmounted by a gilded crest.

"Home at last!" Lord Wye announced. "I want a bath and a good meal, what about you?"

"Is this Wye House?" Elvina asked.

"It is indeed," Lord Wye replied.

The doors were flung open. Footmen in blue livery with gold braid and sparkling buttons came hurrying to the curricle when they saw who occupied it.

A man in a different livery, who Elvina realised was the Major Domo, said in almost scandalised tones,

"Have you brought no groom, my Lord?"

"The fellow was taken sick," Lord Wye replied.

"We have been expecting your Lordship every day for a fortnight," the man remarked in what seemed to Elvina almost a tone of reproach.

"I was delayed, Simpkins," he answered. "Sometime I will tell you about it, but now I need a glass of wine and some food."

He took Elvina by the hand as he spoke and led her into the house.

"I must welcome you to Wye House," he said, "although we are both too tired for pretty speeches."

"Will the young lady be staying here, my Lord?" Simpkins asked in a respectful tone behind their backs.

"Yes, she will be staying. Send Mrs. Maltravers to me."

"Very good, my Lord."

Lord Wye led the way into a large room almost completely lined with books, but looking out on to a formal garden.

It was the most attractive room Elvina had ever seen and although she had no time to note the glittering chandeliers, the polished furniture, the silver sconces and gilt-framed pictures, she had a general impression of luxury and beauty.

"Who is Mrs. – Maltravers?" she asked in a whisper as Simpkins closed the door behind him.

"My housekeeper. She will look after you and must in fact chaperone you until such time as I can procure a lady to act in that capacity."

"To chaperone me?" Elvina asked in dismay.

She knew that it was her kiss that had done this. Never before had he thought of her save as a child. Never before had it troubled him for one moment that conventions were not being observed and proprieties ignored.

"Yes, a chaperone," Lord Wye said sharply. "You must realise, Elvina, that we are now back in the world that takes notice of such things."

He walked across to his writing desk and stared down at a huge pile of letters that lay on it. Beside them Elvina could see stacks of invitation cards.

"We will easily find someone," he went on.

She felt as if with every word he moved further away from her.

"Lady Cleone will doubtless help us."

"I am sure that will not be necessary," Elvina said before she could prevent herself.

"I think you underrate Lady Cleone's kindness," he said coldly. "She has your welfare at heart, I assure you."

Elvina's lips tightened.

Lord Wye looked at her and suddenly, quite unaccountably, he seemed to lose his temper.

"For Heaven's sake don't make it more difficult than it is already. I have promised to look after you and I will keep my promise. What is really wrong is that in circumstances like this I should have a wife. That would solve all our difficulties."

If he had slapped her across the face, Elvina could not have felt more shaken by the blow that he had inflicted on her. Peregrine Howard had told her that she would be an encumbrance and now the truth of it was being brought home.

They had not been five minutes in the house and already insurmountable difficulties were arising.

If she could have spoken, she would have said more, but the door opened and Simpkins appeared followed by a footman bearing a silver tray on which there were several decanters of wine and a number of crystal glasses.

Lord Wye took a glass of wine and drank it as if his thirst were almost unquenchable. Elvina sipped at a glass of Marsala and was almost relieved when a woman dressed in black silk with a white lace cap came quietly into the room to stand respectfully by the door.

"You sent for me, my Lord?" she began.

"Good evening, Mrs. Maltravers." Lord Wye replied. "I want you to look after Miss Elvina, whom I have brought back with me from Portugal. She will be staying with us for a while until I can find her sister who is living somewhere in England. Miss Elvina saved my life, Mrs. Maltravers. It is entirely due to her that I am not at this moment either buried in French soil or rotting in some stinking prison camp."

"Then we are all very grateful to the young lady," Mrs. Maltravers smiled.

"Go with her, Elvina. I shall see you later at dinner," Lord Wye said.

Elvina wanted to run and put her hand upon his arm and to look up into his face and seek reassurances from the kindness of his eyes that she was not an encumbrance.

But because of this strange new restraint between them she could only curtsey politely and follow Mrs. Maltravers from the room.

She was led to a bedroom of such unbelievable luxury that at first she could only stare around her in astonishment.

A big bed hung with white and gold brocade was set against panelled walls painted a soft eggshell blue. There was a blue carpet that Elvina's feet seemed to sink in to almost as if she walked on velvet.

There were gold and silver hangings over the windows and the furniture was carved and gilded and seemed beautiful enough for a Palace rather than a private room.

Elvina saw that her trunk had been brought upstairs and the few gowns that the seamstress had made her in Santander were being hung up in a cupboard by a housemaid in a frilled cap.

"If you are cold, miss, I could light a fire," Mrs. Maltravers offered. "But it has been very warm all day."

"I shall not need a fire, thank you," Elvina said.

"The housemaids are bringing up the water for your bath," Mrs. Maltravers went on.

Elvina saw that a round tub had been placed on one side of the room and beside it were soft white towels, scented soap and a large honeycomb sponge.

"It will be lovely – to have a bath," she sighed. "We have been driving since early morning and I am very dusty."

"Rose will help you," Mrs. Maltravers said, indicating the housemaid who was unpacking Elvina's trunk. "And if there is anything else you want, Rose will come and tell me."

"Thank you," Elvina said.

Mrs. Maltravers withdrew from the room and Elvina looked at Rose who was an apple-cheeked girl a little older than herself. She took off her bonnet, handed it to the maid and began to undress.

She had not got very far before there came a knock at the door.

Rose went to open it and Elvina heard a man's voice tell her something before she closed the door again and came across to the dressing table where Elvina was standing.

"His Lordship's compliments, miss," she said, "and he regrets that, after all, he cannot dine with you tonight. Mr. Simpkins wondered whether you would like dinner downstairs in the dining room or if you would prefer to have a tray up here."

For a moment Elvina could not answer. The disappointment was so intense. At the same time, she almost felt as if she had anticipated it.

"I will have a tray here," she said at length and Rose went to the door to give the order.

Elvina sat down on the chair in front of the dressing table and stared at herself in the silver-framed mirror.

'Was it any wonder he wanted to go out?' she thought to herself. She looked ugly and unattractive. Her skin was so brown, her hair streaked where the dye was wearing off and where the dust of the journey had powdered the waves.

Almost unbidden the picture of Lady Cleone came to her eyes, her magnolia skin, white and unblemished, her dark eyes raised to Lord Wye's face, her little pointed fingers with their beautifully manicured nails fluttering out as if supplicating him to protect and cosset her.

"Rose – I want your help," Elvina said suddenly.

"Of course, miss, if there's anythin' I can do."

"I want some lemons, two or three of them, cucumber , a whole cucumber if you can get it – the white of egg and camomile flowers. Can you get camomile flowers in London?"

"Oh, yes, miss," Rose replied. "Mrs. Maltravers will have some. She always drinks camomile tea when her stomach is upset. She has them packed specially and sent here from his Lordship's house in the country."

"Well, then, some camomile flowers and make an infusion of them in very hot water," Elvina answered.

Mystified but too polite to question this strange request, Rose went away to fetch what she asked for. Elvina undressed and climbed into the bath.

She scrubbed herself all over, washed her hair free of the dust and dirt and then when Rose came back she asked for fresh water and, having washed her hair again, dipped it into the infusion of camomile flowers leaving it to dry.

As she had expected, Juanita's dye had almost worn out its usefulness. Her hair near the roots and on the top of her head became almost as fair as it had been before the night she had escaped from her home.

Only the ends were dark and, asking for a pair of scissors, she cut them off.

Her hair was short, but now it was curling all over her head and around her face. And yet, when she looked in the mirror, she was so dissatisfied with her appearance that she could have cried in disappointment.

The walnut juice must have long been worn away, but the storms they had passed through, the privations she had suffered, the fierce winds and the burning sun had left her skin brown and dark.

She thought of how fair she had been, she looked at the skin on the rest of her body and could have cried at her own ugliness.

Rose had at last realised what she was doing and helped her make an ointment of a white of egg, lemon juice and cucumber and provided too some glycerine, which Mrs. Maltravers used for many homemade remedies.

"Shall I ever get my skin white?" Elvina asked despairingly.

"It will take time, miss, and now you are in England you need not be out in the sun so much. Most ladies carry a sunshade."

"I will start tomorrow," Elvina said with a little smile.

She had her dinner, forcing herself to eat, although, because she was lonely and missed Lord Wye, her appetite seemed to have vanished.

'I must get fatter,' she thought, remembering Lady Cleone's lovely rounded limbs.

She went to bed at length with her fair hair spread out on the pillow like a halo around her little face. She covered her cheeks, her neck and her hands with the lotion and thought, because she was tired, that she would fall asleep at once.

Instead she found herself listening in the darkness for the sound of a man's voice and footsteps coming up the stairs.

Her window overlooked Berkeley Square. She could hear the carriages driving past and more than once she got out of bed and went to the window to see if one stopped outside the front door.

It was not until two o'clock that he came home.

She heard the horses stop, jumped out of bed and had a glimpse of him walking into the house. Very softly she opened her bedroom door.

She heard him say 'goodnight' to the footman on duty.

She heard him come rather heavily up the stairs, walking as a man will who is tired and who has also dined well.

It was through the merest crack that she watched him cross the landing and go to his own room several doors away. She longed to call out to him, longed to run to him, to put her arms up to him and pull his face down to hers.

She loved him, but she was content to remain as a child in his eyes if only he would kiss her cheek, if only he would hold her tight with that affectionate gesture that she knew so well.

And then she knew with an absolute certainty that he would never do it again.

Her kiss had destroyed the child he liked and trusted and she was not yet in a position to replace that affection with anything else.

She went back to bed to lie sleepless, staring with wide eyes into the darkness, her brain turning over and over again the problem that sshe could find, at the moment, no solution for.

In the morning she saw that the lotion she had placed on her face had helped a little, but not as much as she would have liked. The sunburn was still there, but now in contrast her hair seemed very fair.

It was only six o'clock when she awoke, but, as she was so used to rising early, she stared at herself in the mirror while the pale sunshine flooded the room and shimmered on her hair.

It was then, in that moment, that she knew what she must do. She could not let him see her like this.

It was perhaps the locket lying on the dressing table where she had left it the night before that gave her the solution to the problem that had kept her awake all night.

She picked it up and stared at the lovely pictured face of her mother, the fair hair, the white skin, the delicate blush in the cheeks, the soft pink of her lips. How lovely she had been!

She placed it round her neck and dressed herself quickly. She wrapped herself in the cape that she had worn for travelling and put the same chip straw bonnet over her hair that she had worn the night before.

Then she hesitated for a moment before going to the writing table and picking up the big white quill pen.

For a moment she stared down at the writing paper with its engraved crest.

Then she began to write.

> "*My Lord,*
>> *I think I know where I can find my sister. I have gone there and will return to tell you everything in a short space of time.*
>> *Please do not forget me and the happy times we have had together. I am quite safe and I beg you not to worry about me but to remember me for I could never forget you.*
> *Elvina.*"

She wrote the letter and sealed it with a wafer and then, holding it in her hands, laid it against her heart.

It was a desperate gamble that she was about to do and yet, because she was a woman and because she was in love, she knew that only by taking a great risk would she ever attain what she most desired.

She thought of Lady Cleone and her lips tightened. She was leaving the field open and yet, if Lord Wye cared for her at all, would he not worry?

Would not Lady Cleone's arrival in London be overshadowed by his anxiety?

She left the letter on the writing desk and opened the door.

The house was quiet save in some room not so far away she could hear a housemaid drawing back the curtains.

Swiftly and on tiptoe she slipped down the stairs. There was no one in the hall, but she could hear a footman speaking to another on the other side of a baize door.

It took her a few minutes to discover how to lift the chain, turn the key and the handle and then the door was open and she was outside in the sunshine.

She drew a deep breath. London was big and already the streets seemed to her to be full. She could hear the postman's bell and the crossing sweepers were already in position, hoping that the first passers-by would reward them for their pains.

For one moment Elvina felt panic sweep over her and she wanted to run back into the house. She wanted to rush to Lord Wye's side, to fall on her knees beside him.

She wanted to tell him that she loved him, that she could not live, not even for a little while, without him.

And then the sight of an elegant carriage moving through the streets made her think once more of Lady Cleone.

This was her only hope, the only way that she could fight equally for Lord Wye's heart.

Resolutely she walked away, conscious that several passers-by stared at her a little curiously.

She was frightened and yet, when she stopped the Postman, her voice was quite steady.

"Excuse me – please," she said. "Can you direct me to the nearest Post Office?"

"That I can, miss," the Postman answered. "'Tis just around the corner in Mount Street. On the left hand side you'll find it."

"Thank you very much."

She set off in the direction that he had pointed out to her.

It only took her two or three minutes to find the Post Office and she went up to a rather austere-looking man in charge.

"Will you be kind enough," she said, "to give me the address of Lord Clanwarren?"

CHAPTER ELEVEN

Lord Wye awoke in one of his moods.

"When 'is Lordship has a fit of the sullens," his valet said to Mrs. Maltravers, "I keeps me mouth shut and says nothin'."

Breakfast was eaten in gloomy silence and then Lord Wye hurried out of the house as if he had an important engagement.

As a matter of fact he was not due at Carlton House until noon, but he was anxious not to see Elvina and he wished, above all things, not to face up to the question that hovered at the back of his mind and which, try as he could, he could not evade.

It was a hot day with a sultry warmth that made the streets seem almost stifling.

Most of the *Beau Monde* had already left London for their country seats but, owing to the news from Spain, the Prince Regent was still at Carlton House so as to be in close touch with the Prince Minister, which meant that 'Prinny's set' at any rate were forced to remain in the Capital.

Lord Wye met various acquaintances on his way up Berkeley Street, who all expressed surprise at seeing him.

"Thought you were in Portugal, old boy," one of them remarked. "Did the black-eyed señoritas turn out disappointing?"

He was astonished when Lord Wye, instead of laughing at his joke, scowled at him ferociously and muttering something uncomplimentary strode away.

"What maggot's got into Wye's head?" he asked his friend before they resumed their walk.

Lord Wye went to White's Club, which he found practically empty as it was so early in the morning. He sat himself down at a writing table, but found himself quite unable to begin a letter of any sort.

Instead he found himself thinking of Elvina.

He could see her as she was the first moment he set eyes on her in his yacht, the fear in her eyes as she pleaded with him and those hazel-green eyes that seemed, he thought, almost to have a hypnotic power where he was concerned.

He could not forget them and could not evade his thoughts of her.

That moment in the storm when he had found her clinging to the table leg, the courage she had jumped with from the porthole to swim ashore, the way that she had procured him a French soldier's uniform and then their long struggle to remain unobserved in the wake of the French Army.

Could any other child, or woman for that matter, have been so courageous under such extraordinary circumstances?

He could feel her little hands in his now, as he had dragged her over the rough roads. Her feet must have been in agony. She must often have been tired to the point of complete exhaustion and yet she had never complained.

He thought of the trusting way that she had slept close beside him, one hand holding onto his jacket as if she was afraid that he would escape her.

He could remember the lightness of her body when he carried her through the fog.

He threw down his pen and rang the bell for the waiter.

"Bring me a brandy," he ordered curtly.

"Very good, my Lord."

The brandy did not help.

He went on seeing pictures and feeling the ghost of what had been enfolding him, whispering in his ear and touching him with soft lips.

"*Kiss me goodnight!*"

He could hear his own voice saying it in that dim dirty shack where they had slept at St. Jean Pied de Port. He was aware that she hesitated and then she had moved towards him.

He could hardly see her face, but he had known that her eyes were on him. Then he felt her cheek soft and warm against his. He had laughed and put out his arms to draw her down to him.

"What sort of kiss do you call that?" he asked. "A butterfly one? Or is it the touch of a little grey moth that is frightened of the dark?"

He both heard and felt her laugh for his arms were around her and her face was only a few inches away from his.

"This is no life for a child," he had said as much to himself as to her. "One day I will teach you to play. I will give you all the things you deserve instead of potatoes and dry bread."

"They were delicious!"

She was laughing again and he loved her for it.

"Shall we plan the meal we will have when we reach London?" he asked.

"In England it would have to be roast beef and apple pie," she teased.

"We eat other things as well," he answered, "but both those would seem an epicurean feast at this moment."

"Talk about something else," she suggested sensibly, "it only makes us hungry."

"And what do you suggest?" he enquired.

"A comfortable bed, clean white linen sheets or perhaps a bath in warm water."

It was his turn to laugh.

"I had forgotten how dirty and disreputable we must look. If my friends in St. James's could see me now, I swear they would never recognise me! But now we must go to sleep."

She wondered why he was suddenly anxious to end their conversation. Was it because he had mentioned his friends in St. James's?

"Goodnight, Elvina."

He waited, but she did not bend her head and kiss him so he did not take his arms away from her.

"Goodnight." Her voice was very low and sweet. "Sleep – well."

"Goodnight," he said again and waited.

Then suddenly, as if she understood, she bent her head and pressed her lips against his cheek.

"That's better."

He had kissed her in return. Her lips were like peach blossom against his cheek. She had a faint sweet fragrance about her that reminded him of jasmine.

Then, without his realising it, she was free of his encircling arms. He heard her snuggle down on the dry leaves and felt a sudden contentment seep over him.

It was a feeling so strong and so vivid that now he knew that it must have been happiness.

He filled his glass half-full with brandy and then, with an oath that came strangely even to his own ears, for he was not a swearing man, he threw the goblet into the fireplace and heard it shatter into a thousand pieces.

"What has happened, my Lord?"

The waiter's surprised voice recalled him to his senses.

"It slipped out of my hand," he said sharply. "Put it on my bill."

"Very good, my Lord."

Lord Wye turned on his heel and walked from the Club down St. James's Street. He was frowning and several cronies who lifted their hats to him were astonished to obtain no response.

He reached Carlton House nearly half an hour early and was kept clicking his heels in an antechamber until the Prince Regent was ready to receive him.

He lunched with the Prince Regent and afterwards was sent in his carriage to Downing Street where he had a long audience with the Prime Minister, putting forward the Prince Regent's suggestions for the future conduct of the War.

"Do you, my Lord, think any of these ideas are in the least practical?" the Prime Minister enquired.

"I cannot see Wellington agreeing to any of them," Lord Wye replied with a smile.

The Prime Minister smiled back.

"Thank the Prince Regent for his most admirable and helpful ideas and say that every one of them will be considered very carefully at the War Office."

"I doubt if His Royal Highness will be satisfied with that," Lord Wye commented.

"Then you will have to convince him," the Prime Minister replied.

He sighed and held out his hand.

"Thank God you are back, Wye. The Prince Regent has been at me night and day to do this and to do that and, when I had to cope with him, my wife said that I was as near a madman as she had ever seen, with the exception of His Majesty!"

"I will do my best," Lord Wye said, with so much heaviness in his voice that the Prime Minister looked at him sharply.

"You seem a bit under the weather. For Heaven's sake don't overtax yourself. We must not forget that you have been through some pretty gruelling experiences in the Peninsular. You had best spend a few days at your country house. Persuade the Prince Regent to go to Brighthelmstone and take Lady Hertford with him. That should keep him occupied. The trouble is that without you none of us can persuade him to do anything."

"You flatter me," Lord Wye replied.

He did not seem particularly pleased with the compliment.

"What is the matter?" the Prime Minister asked him.

His voice had a fatherly note in it. He was genuinely fond of the handsome young Peer facing him.

"Nothing, nothing," Lord Wye answered. "Nothing at any rate that I need trouble you with."

"It would be no trouble," the Prime Minister said, suddenly yearning for his confidence.

"No one can help me at the moment. I have a decision to make, that is all, and I think I have made it. I intend to get married."

The Prime Minister was all smiles. So that was all that was wrong with the boy. He was lovesick! Ah, well. that was understandable at his age.

"My congratulations," he said genially. "I can imagine nothing that would give your friends greater pleasure. May I know the name of the lucky lady?"

"I think I had best tell her myself first," Lord Wye answered.

"Tell her from me she would be a fool to refuse you," the Prime Minister insisted.

"Oh, she is not likely to do that," Lord Wye replied.

He went from the study closing the door behind him.

The Prime Minister stood looking after him for nearly a full minute.

'There is something wrong,' he thought, scratching his chin, and yet there was little he could do about it.

If the girl of his choice would accept Lord Wye, then what was amiss? Why the scowls? The note of depression in his voice?

The Prime Minister pondered on this problem but found no answer. Then he settled himself again at his desk and the affairs of State commanded all his concentration.

Lord Wye drove back to Carlton House in the Prince Regent's carriage, delivered the Prime Minister's message, then made his excuses and went back to White's.

He was determined somehow to fill the day and to put off the evil hour when he must return home to face Elvina.

He was afraid to face the consequences of the decision he had made in the Prime Minister's house.

He sat down to a game of faro and, having won by sheer irresponsible play, five thousand guineas, told an attendant to collect the money for him and strode from the gambling room without even saying 'goodnight'.

"What's the matter with Wye?" someone asked. "He looks as if the Devil was at his heels!"

'The Devil is not at my heels but inside me,' Lord Wye thought, overhearing the remark. And now at last he realised that he could run away no longer and, settling himself behind a newspaper, he forced himself to think.

It was no use going round and round the question. It was there confronting him. What was he going to do about Elvina?

He knew now that the plans he made so light-heartedly of keeping her with him until he found her sister, of being her patron and her protector so long as she needed him, were quite impossible.

The kiss they had exchanged so inadvertently in the curricle had changed everything. Even now, as he looked back at it, he could hardly believe it was true.

Yet it was impossible to forget that sudden tingling ecstasy that had run through his veins, the sudden leaping flame of passion that had startled him with its very violence until he had jerked away loathing and despising himself, knowing that he was lower and more despicable than the drunken Frenchmen who had roamed St. Jean Pied de Port crying, 'bring out your women!'

How it could have happened he had no idea. But it had and therefore everything was changed.

'A child! A child of thirteen, but she seems so like a young woman,' he muttered to himself, and called so loudly for brandy that several of the older members looked up in disapproval.

'I must send her away,' Lord Wye told himself and then wondered if he would ever have the courage to do so.

He knew only too well the expression there would be in Elvina's hazel-green eyes.

He could almost feel her little fingers clutching at his arm and the sob in her voice that he had heard before when she had begged him to keep her with him and not to leave her behind in Portugal.

'*Please take me! Please – please!*'

He felt something almost like a thrill go through him and turned it into a shiver. Was he a monster that he could feel like this for a mere child?

Someone came in through the door at the end of the room. He heard his own name mentioned and looked up to see the handsome rather bored face of Peregrine Howard.

He knew then that this was what he had been waiting for, the arrival of the woman he would marry and he had already spoken about her to the Prime Minister.

Lord Wye rose to his feet.

"You have travelled quickly, Peregrine."

"Not as quickly as you."

"When did you arrive?"

"About two hours ago. Cleone asked me to come and find you. She particularly wants to see you."

"I am honoured by her thought."

"She is at our aunt's house in Curzon Street. My carriage is outside."

Feeling as if he was acting in a play and already knew the part, Lord Wye let Peregrine Howard lead him to where an elegant carriage was standing outside the Club.

"You must have found some good horseflesh to come here at such speed," Lord Wye commented.

Peregrine laughed.

"When Cleone sets her heart on anything, she always has her own way. She persuaded an old fellow who lives near

Southampton to lend us a coach and four for the first part of our journey. After that we were fortunate or perhaps the posting houses were as much impressed with Cleone's beauty as with my money."

"An irresistible combination I am sure," Lord Wye replied with a note of sarcasm in his voice.

He found Peregrine Howard's fulsome praise of his sister somewhat irritating. He was never quite certain whether he was really as besotted by her beauty as he appeared to be or was putting on an act so that other people should never forget even for a moment.

The house in Curzon Street was redolent with the scent of lilies and the sun blinds over the windows made the rooms shadowy as well as cool.

Lady Cleone, in a diaphanous garment that revealed rather than concealed her figure, was reclining on a *chaise longue*.

She stretched out her hand to welcome Lord Wye, but did not rise from the silken cushions that supported her. There were faint lines of weariness under her eyes, but she was looking exceedingly lovely.

Lord Wye kissed her hand.

"May I welcome you to London?"

"I am so delighted to see you," she answered. "I was half-afraid that you would already have left for the country and then I remembered that both the Prince Regent and the Prime Minister would be in need of you, so I hoped that you would still be here."

"I have transacted all my business with both the gentlemen you have just mentioned," Lord Wye replied, "so now I can be wholly at your service as long as you want me."

He was aware as he was speaking that Peregrine had withdrawn discreetly from the room.

He and Lady Cleone were alone in the soft light

The lilies were almost overpowering but Lord Wye was not certain whether the fragrance came from the vases of flowers on the tables or from Lady Cleone herself.

"I thought of you all the way to London," she said in a soft voice. "I spoke to Peregrine of your bravery and of all you have been through. We both felt that we had not told you sufficiently how much we admire you."

"You make me feel embarrassed. I did nothing but what circumstances forced me to do."

"A lesser man would have given up and would have surrendered himself to the inevitable," Lady Cleone said. "But you struggled on."

"Elvina would let me do little else," Lord Wye answered.

The name was spoken between them. It slipped out involuntarily, but now it was spoken he felt the significance of what he had said and knew too that Lady Cleone had stiffened.

He rose suddenly and walked to the window. A carriage passed drawn by two elegant chestnut horses, a man rode by on a grey stallion and Lord Wye wondered who the next person would be and knew that his thoughts were playing for time.

'Go on, you fool,' he told himself. 'Propose to her. Get it over. Ask her to be your wife. She is willing enough, you know that.'

He had a sudden fancy that it was Elvina who was drawing him back, pulling at him with her little hands and pleading with him through trembling lips.

'Don't do it. *Don't,*' she was saying.

Almost roughly he thrust her aside.

'I must. There is nothing else I can do.'

'Don't! *Don't!* It will be too late. I must stop you! Can you not see? *I must!*'

He shook himself free of his fantasies.

He turned towards the *chaise longue*.

"Cleone," he tried to say, but her name seemed strangled in his throat. "I want to speak to you about – Elvina."

Her voice came to him with a sudden hard note in it that he had not noticed before. He had a sense of panic lest she should know about that kiss, the kiss that had altered everything that lay between him and Elvina.

"What did you want to say?"

His question was apprehensive and his voice almost unsteady.

"I thought it would be best, while you look for Elvina's sister, that we should send her to stay with my old Nanny in Oxfordshire. She is a decent woman and would look after the child properly. You need not be afraid of her coming to any harm and you would be free of the inconvenience of having her at Berkeley Square."

"The inconvenience?"

The question seemed to tear itself from Lord Wye's lips.

"But, of course," Lady Cleone said with one of her polished smiles. "What can a bachelor know of the needs of a child? How can a bachelor household accommodate someone of Elvina's age without altering the whole routine of how the house is run?"

She paused for a moment and then, looking at Lord Wye standing a little apart from her, she said,

"Of course if you was married, it would be very different."

Her dark eyelashes fell, sweeping her cheeks. She portrayed, most admirably, a picture of pretty confusion and Lord Wye knew that this was his cue.

Yet something made it impossible for him to speak.

He had only to take one step forward. He had only to say the words that Lady Cleone was waiting to hear and he knew that he would be a betrothed man.

"If I was married, "he asked and even to himself his voice seemed to come from far away, "do you imagine that my wife would welcome Elvina?"

Lady Cleone gave a little laugh.

"She could at least take the trouble of her off your hands," she replied. "That is after all what wives are for, to save a man trouble when it comes to dealing with such tiresome things as other people's children."

"You think a wife would do that?"

Lord Wye's voice was solemn.

"But, of course," Lady Cleone went on, "Elvina will doubtless find her sister and, if the sister does not exist, which I am beginning to suspect, then she should be put in a Seminary and educated. Indeed I know just the place. It specialises in taking the daughters of impoverished gentlefolk. The girls are educated, brought up properly and then found employment. They become Governesses and companions and Elvina would, I assure you, fare well there."

Lord Wye was silent and Lady Cleone held out her hand to him.

"Come and sit near me," she suggested. "We are wasting precious time in discussing your little Portuguese protégée when we might be talking about ourselves. Don't give her another thought, I beg of you. I will see to everything. She can go to my old Nanny and then at the beginning of the term I myself will take her to Mrs. Dawson's Seminary. Now is your mind at rest?"

"And why are you doing all this?"

Lord Wye's question seemed to echo around the room.

He had not moved one step towards Lady Cleone and yet she appeared unaware of his reticence, her hand remaining outstretched towards him.

Now the other one came out to join it, white fluttering little hands with long thin fingers and polished nails.

And her beautiful face tilted up to his was very alluring.

"Are you really so stupid?" she asked softly, "Do you not know the answer to that question."

"Yes, I think I do know the answer," Lord Wye replied. "I am sorry, Cleone, but I cannot do it."

Her hands fell, palms downwards into her lap.

"Cannot do what? What do you mean?"

Her voice was hard.

"I cannot marry you," Lord Wye said.

"Why not?

"Because I love Elvina. I have fought against it and tried to hide the fact even from myself," Lord Wye answered. "But I love her."

"You are insane! You cannot love her. She is only a child!"

"She will grow up," he replied. "I shall send her to school. Not to the Seminary you suggest for Governesses and companions, but to the best school in the land. And when she is old enough, I shall marry her."

"Marry a Portuguese brat with no parents, no breeding and no background!" Lady Cleone screamed. "Do you think that will make you happy? You fool! When I was ready, yes, I confess it, to give myself to you."

"I am very sensible of the honour that you would have accorded me," Lord Wye said with a note of sarcasm in his voice. "Although I think, Cleone, we can be frank with each other, you and I. You would not marry me if I was a penniless soldier without wealth or title."

"Why should I throw myself away on anyone in such circumstances?" Lady Cleone asked, her eyes flashing.

"Why should you indeed," Lord Wye replied. "Yet, if she loved such a man, Elvina would."

He said the words gently and for the first time since the argument started he moved.

He walked towards the *chaise longue* and stood looking down at the woman who sat there, her eyes blazing with anger and her breasts heaving.

"Goodbye, Cleone," he said. "I think, if you ask me, we have both had a lucky escape."

"You are mad enough for Bedlam!" Lady Cleone spat at him. "You will be sorry for this. But don't say I did not warn you!"

"I will not," Lord Wye retorted.

He lifted her hand perfunctorily to his lips and then, as she snatched it petulantly away, walked across the room and out of her life.

He therefore did not see Lady Cleone beat her hands against the silk pillows and throw them one by one onto the floor.

It was only a short step to Berkeley Square and Lord Wye almost ran the distance.

Quite suddenly the way was clear before him.

His doubts and fears and miseries were gone. He wondered why he had been so stupid as not to have thought of this solution before.

He would explain everything to Elvina.

Gently, of course, so as not to frighten her, not mentioning the kiss and what it had done to him, letting her believe that the love she had shown him so ardently and so unashamedly was reciprocated in a like manner by his devotion and affection for her.

Dear little Elvina! He felt his whole being surge out towards her.

He wanted to be with her again, to see the happiness in her smile and to see her eyes light up as he came into the room.

She would understand why he had been away so long. She at least made no demands upon a man. She had only ever asked for one thing – that she might be with him and that he would not desert her.

One day they would be together forever. He would tell her that. It would be something for them both to live for.

He tried not to think that four years was a long time. He could marry her at seventeen, perhaps a few months earlier. But, even so, it was a long wait and they would both have to be very brave about it.

"Elvina! *Elvina!*"

He said her name aloud and, hurrying to his own front door, beat upon the knocker impatiently because the footman on duty did not open the door as quickly as he wished.

He handed his hat to Simpkins.

"Bring some wine to the study," he ordered, "and tell Miss Elvina that I wish to see her immediately."

He did not wait for an answer, but went into what he always thought of as his room.

He could remember Elvina looking round it last night when they had come there and he had known that she had been a little overawed by the magnificence of everything.

And yet, by her very unselfconsciousness, by her grace and by the way she always seemed to know how to do the right thing, she had not appeared gauche or in any way alien to such surroundings.

Lord Wye almost snorted aloud. Let Lady Cleone say what she liked with her bitter tongue. Elvina was well bred.

All the time they had been together he had never seen her do anything that was not an action of distinctive good taste.

"I beg your pardon, my Lord."

"What is it, Simpkins?"

"Miss Elvina is not here!"

"Not here? What do you mean?"

"She went out, my Lord."

"Alone! And you let her?"

"I am afraid I knew nothing about it, my Lord. She left first thing this morning, before your Lordship was called."

"She left the house? How could she have done so? Who authorised such a thing? Send Mrs. Maltravers to me at once."

"She has been waiting to see you, my Lord. The young lady left a note behind."

"Then bring it to me! For God's sake, man, bring it to me! What are we waiting for?"

It seemed to Lord Wye that he waited for almost an interminable time before Mrs. Maltravers appeared.

She came rustling into the room in her black gown and held out to him the note that Elvina had left on the writing table.

Lord Wye took it from her.

He broke the wafer and some other part of himself noted that his hands were trembling.

He read what Elvina had written. Read it once and then again before he said in a voice that he hardly recognised as his own,

"Where did she go? What orders did she give to the carriage?"

"She did not take one, my Lord, as far as we know," Mrs. Maltravers answered. "The footman found the front door open, so she must have unbolted it herself."

"Where could she have gone? She knew no one in London."

"She does not say in the note, my Lord?"

"No, of course she does not or I should not be asking you," Lord Wye snapped and then, seeing Mrs. Maltraver's face, added, "I am sorry, believe me. I am overwrought and worried. She is only a child, Mrs. Maltravers. She has never been in London before. What will become of her?"

"She will not have gone to any relations, my Lord?"

"She would not know where they are. There were no messages for her? No one called?"

"No, my Lord."

"Then I must find out about her sister." Lord Wye declared. "She has one, I know. She is married to a man named Thompson, Captain Thompson."

He turned and glanced at the clock over the mantelpiece.

"The War Office will be closed now. It will be useless for me to go there before the morning. Question the household, Mrs. Maltravers. See if anyone, anyone at all, saw Miss Elvina leave this morning."

"I think Simpkins has already done that, my Lord, but I will do it again," Mrs. Maltravers said.

She curtseyed and would have left the room had not something in Lord Wye's face prompted her to say,

"She seems a very sweet young lady, my Lord. Rose says she spoke most gently and kindly to her and was very grateful for everything that was done for her comfort. We should all be very upset if anything should happen to her."

"Upset!" Lord Wye said. "It will be more than that, Mrs. Maltravers. Miss Elvina is – "

He paused for a moment before he finished very distinctly,

" – everything in the world to me."

CHAPTER TWELVE

"He is coming!"

The old lady in the window held up a letter in triumph towards her elderly husband standing by the mantelshelf.

"Is he, by gad!" Lord Clanwarren exclaimed. "You must have used your wiles on him, My dear. Or did you tell him the truth?"

Lady Clanwarren chuckled.

"I told him that I had something of import to communicate, which I believed would be of interest to him."

Lord Clanwarren said nothing for a moment and then in an unexpectedly gruff voice he remarked,

"And supposing he is not interested?"

His wife clasped her hands together.

"As if I had not thought of that," she said in a worried tone. "Just suppose that the poor sweet child has been all through this for nothing. I cannot bear to think of such a thing."

"We may have to face it," Lord Clanwarren replied.

"I know, I know," his wife agreed. "But I cannot believe that his Lordship's heart is not a little inclined towards her. I know he only saw her in rags and with that awful walnut juice on her skin. Oh, the horror of that dye! I thought we should have to skin the poor little love before it finally came away and left her as white and beautiful as God intended her to be."

"Like her mother," Lord Clanwarren answered almost beneath his breath. "Yes, George, like my darling Sybil.

Sometimes I forget and think that she is back with us again."

Lord Clanwarren walked across the room to lay his hand on his wife's shoulder.

"It was my fault, my dear. I ought never to have driven her away. I have regretted it always, but my damned pride would not let me say so."

"No, no, George. You are not to torture yourself," Lady Clanwarren cried, putting out her hands towards him in a protective gesture. "Sybil was very foolish, but she was young and innocent and that man swept her off her feet."

"That swine! I would wring his neck if he was here."

"I don't think, from what Elvina has told me, that we could wish him anything worse than what he has inflicted on himself," Lady Clanwarren said. "If you could only see the poor child's back. It's still scarred by the whippings that wicked woman gave her."

"If I was a younger man," Lord Clanwarren asserted. "I would go out to Portugal, tell them both what I think of them and see that they got their deserts."

"No, no, leave them alone. It's all over now, Elvina is with us and safe. It's only that alas her heart is elsewhere."

"What do we know about this fellow, Wye?" Lord Clanwarren inquired. "His father was a decent fellow, I remember him. But young Wye may be a waster for all we know."

"No, no, my dear, people speak most highly of him, and Elvina loves him. That is what really matters."

"I should have thought that it was more important to ask whether he loves her," Lord Clanwarren replied.

His wife rose to her feet

"If anything was to go wrong for Elvina now," she said with a quaver in her voice, "I don't think I could bear it. That is why I wrote to him. George, did I do wrong?"

"No, no, my dear, I am certain you did right. 'Twas a little risky though."

"I felt that the child had to know the best or the worst," Lady Clanwarren replied. "I know that she has been thinking of him day after day, struggling to make herself beautiful. And now she is afraid, yes, afraid, George to face him for fear that his affections are already engaged elsewhere."

"How do you know all this?" Lord Clanwarren enquired.

"From what she has told me I know too that she has sat up night after night composing a letter to him, only when morning has come to tear up everything she has written."

"So you took matters into your own hands," Lord Clanwarren said quietly.

"Yes, George. You don't think I have made a mistake?"

"I have never known your instinct at fault," he replied gallantly.

She gushed a little and raised her face to his with a pretty gesture. He was just dropping a kiss on her cheek when the door opened and they both turned to see Elvina come hurrying into the room.

"Grandmama!" she called in her sweet voice. "I have been down to the stables and Foxhunter has a foal. Is it not very exciting?"

"It is indeed my love," Lady Clanwarren answered, turning towards her granddaughter with a look of deep affection on her face.

"I had no idea that foals could be so gay and skittish from the moment they are born," Elvina said. "And, Grandpapa!

Johnston says that I can ride Clarion today. Will you take me out with you this afternoon?"

"Not this afternoon, my dear," Lord Clanwarren answered. "We have a visitor."

"How disappointing!" Elvina exclaimed.

"Tomorrow morning," he suggested. "That is if you still want to go with me."

"As if I should want to do anything else," Elvina replied fondly.

She smiled from one to the other of the old people and held out a hand to both of them with a pretty impulsive gesture that touched both their hearts.

"You are so kind to me," she said. "It is so wonderful to be here, to see the things that were my mother's and to know that I belong."

"You are happy, my darling?" Lady Clanwarren asked.

There was just a moment's pause before Elvina responded,

"Very, very happy, if only – "

She stopped suddenly but her grandmother knew how the sentence would have ended.

An elderly woman in a mobcap came into the salon carrying a silver salver on which reposed a large glass of milk.

"Your milk. Miss Elvina," she said.

"Oh, not more milk!" Elvina cried. "I swear if I drink another glass, I shall turn into a cow! Besides, I am so fat already that my new gowns will have to be let out even before I have worn them."

"That is a very pretty frock you are wearing now," Lord Clanwarren remarked looking down at the sprigged muslin with pale blue ribbons that became Elvina's white skin and fair hair.

It made her look as sweet and fresh as a flower opening to the first rays of the sun.

"They are all lovely!" she exclaimed.

"Your milk, Miss Elvina," the old woman insisted.

"Nanny, you are a bully," Elvina pouted, but taking the glass of milk she drank it down.

"It is delicious," she said. "I ought not to complain. When I think of the thin blue stuff that we called milk in Portugal, I could drink great buckets of this for the sheer delight of tasting the cream."

"We hope you will," Lady Clanwarren said.

"Then I shall be so fat that you will be ashamed of me!"

"I don't think you could ever be that," her grandmother said, looking at her delicate fairylike features and the young, still too slender body that was, however, filling out.

"You grow more like your mother every day," Lord Clanwarren observed.

"Indeed, she does, my Lord," Nanny agreed, "though it was hard to see the resemblance the night she arrived here. I shall never forget my first glimpse of her.

"'Who's that servant girl at the door?' I says to old Newman.

"I happened to be passing through the hall and saw her. It was getting dusk or I might have looked closer.

"'Somebody for her Ladyship,' Newman answered.

"'Her Ladyship's tired,' I says, quite snappy-like.

"Then the servant girl, for I swear I thought she was nothing else, takes a locket from round her neck and holds it out to me.

"'Will you take this to either Lord or Lady Clanwarren,' she says in her pretty voice. I has one look at it.

"''Tis Miss Sybil!' I cries. 'My own dear baby that was!'

"And then I takes another look at the child and feels my legs begin to shake.

"'And who be you?' I asks."

Elvina gave a little laugh.

They had all heard the story a dozen times, but it seemed as if none of them could hear it too often.

"'I am – Elvina,' I said, did I not, Nanny?"

"That's what you said," the old woman answered with tears in her eyes. "And you added, 'my mother was called Sybil'."

"Oh, Grandmama! It was exciting, was it not?" Elvina said. "When Nanny brought me in here and you were sitting by the fireside with Grandpapa opposite you and you looked up in surprise – and Nanny started saying who I was and showing you the locket."

"And the ring," Nanny interposed. "The ring that Miss Sybil had worn since her twelfth birthday! I remembers her Ladyship giving it to her. She was that excited it might have been made of diamonds."

"It has meant far more to me than if it had been made of all the most precious stones in the world," Elvina said. "That and the locket were all I had of Mama's for so many years and now you have given me – so many things of hers."

"You shall have many more, my darling," Lady Clanwarren promised.

Elvina wiped a tear from her eye.

"You are making me cry and I must not cry because I want to look so nice for you. Have you noticed that the last roughness has gone from my skin? I really am white at last. When I look in the mirror I can hardly recognise myself."

"You are very pretty, my dear," Lord Clanwarren enthused.

"That is what I wanted you to say," Elvina said with a twinkle in her eyes.

Then her smile faded.

"Do you really think I look pretty, Grandpapa? Really and truly?"

"But, of course," he answered. "Are you vain enough to want me to repeat it?"

"I just wanted to make sure," Elvina explained, "that – a man would think so."

Lady Clanwarren met her husband's eyes across Elvina's head.

"Dearest," she said, "will you do something for me?"

"But, of course. Grandmama. Anything you wish."

"Then, as we have a visitor this afternoon, would you be kind enough to cut me some roses for the vase on my writing desk? I know many of them are over, but there are still one or two white blooms at the very end of the Rose Garden by the water lily pond."

"But of course, Grandmama. I will go and get them at once."

"That would be very kind, my dear."

"Come on, Nanny. Come and help me," Elvina replied.

"No, indeed, miss! I have other things to do. Your gown to finish for tonight for one."

"That new one of white gauze? Oh, I am longing to wear it. Will it really be finished?"

"There is only the hem to be turned up," Nanny answered.

Elvina raised herself on tiptoe and kissed the old woman's cheek.

"I can never thank you enough for making me look like myself again," she said. "At times I felt I could hardly bear the pain of the herbs and lotions that you rubbed on my skin to take the dye away. But now when I look in a mirror I want to shout for joy!"

Before Nanny could answer she had run from the room and for a moment it seemed to the three people watching her go that the sunshine had gone with her.

"Must we lose her to some damned fellow so soon after we have found her?" Lord Clanwarren asked.

"She loves him," his wife replied and he heard the pain in her voice. "She seems gay and happy when she is with us, but Nanny tells me that night after night she cries into her pillow and often, when she thinks we don't see, she sits staring into space, her thoughts only of him, her whole being yearning for him."

"Suppose he is not the man she believes him to be?" Lord Clanwarren asked fiercely.

"We can only pray," his wife replied.

"She has more chance than her mother had," Nanny said, her voice breaking in on them almost harshly. "Child she may be in some ways, but she is old in others. She has been through a great deal and she would not be taken in by a bad man, as my poor baby was."

"If he is not a decent sort, I swear to you that I will not stand by and see her suffer," Lord Clanwarren vowed harshly. "I will turn the fellow out of this house neck and crop. After all he is not the only man in the world."

The door was flung open and the butler announced,

"Lord Wye, my Lady!"

They all turned to see who had come into the room. In silence they watched him walk towards them, a tall, broad-shouldered, handsome young man dressed in the height of fashion.

Yet there was something singularly unfashionable about the way that he moved, hurriedly and purposefully, as if time was of importance and he could not bear to linger.

Nanny moved respectfully into the background as Lord Wye reached Lady Clanwarren and bowed over her hand.

"Your Ladyship must accept my apologies for being earlier than was intended," he said in a deep attractive voice. "I know that in your most kind invitation you asked me for four o'clock. But I could not wait, I had to hear what it was you wished to impart to me."

"You are welcome at any hour, my Lord," Lady Clanwarren smiled politely. "I don't think you have met my husband."

"Your father was a friend of mine," Lord Clanwarren added, holding out his hand.

"I often heard him speak of you, my Lord," Lord Wye replied. "I have, in fact, myself long regretted that, although we are comparatively close neighbours, I have not availed myself of the opportunity of making your acquaintance."

"It is remedied now," Lady Clanwarren said with a smile. "Will not your Lordship be seated?"

"You will forgive me if I seem importunate," Lord Wye said. "But in your note your Ladyship said you had something to impart to me."

Looking up into his face, Lady Clanwarren was struck by the eagerness in his eyes and the whole feeling of tension about him. She realised that here was no soft-lived hanger-on at Court, as she had been half-afraid.

There was wiriness and a hardness about Lord Wye that belied the fashionable cut of his clothes.

There was a sharpness about his features as if he had been driving himself hard these past weeks and there were lines under his eyes as if he had lost a great deal of sleep.

"I have indeed something to show you that may well be of interest to you," she said quietly.

She moved across the room to seat herself in a high-backed chair beside the fireplace. Lord Clanwarren followed her, but, although he too sat down and indicated with his hand that another chair was available, Lord Wye still stood.

"Perhaps your Ladyship has some idea of what I am seeking," he said, and she knew by the impatient note in his voice that the polite preliminaries were irksome for him.

"I am afraid my husband and I live very much out of the world," Lady Clanwarren said. "It would be kind if your Lordship would explain."

"It is a girl who is lost," Lord Wye said, "or rather a child. I brought her home to England from Portugal, and incidentally, she saved my life, but when we arrived in London, she left my house early one morning and has not been seen again."

"You have tried to find her?" Lord Clanwarren asked, his eyes from under his bristling eyebrows searching Lord Wye's face.

"I have scoured the length and breadth of England for her," Lord Wye answered. "She told me that her sister was married to a Captain Thompson of the English Army. I have been through every record at the War Office. I have visited dozens of Thompsons, but not one of them was married to a Portuguese wife. I have had the Bow Street Runners out. I have even offered a reward for information as to her whereabouts."

"A reward!" Lord Clanwarren exclaimed. "And how much did you consider a reasonable sum for the finding of this, er, this child?"

"Twenty thousand pounds," Lord Wye replied.

"Twenty thousand pounds!"

The sum seemed to take Lord Clanwarren's breath away. He could only repeat the words while Lady Clanwarren clasped her blue-veined hands together.

"She must – mean very – much to you, my Lord," she faltered.

"She means everything in the world," Lord Wye answered. "Everything! I have to find her. Can you understand? I have to find her. And I am growing desperate."

"You have no clue as to her whereabouts?" Lord Clanwarren enquired.

"None," Lord Wye answered. "I have been everywhere, I have done everything that was humanly possible. But she has vanished! Vanished! And now, unless you can help me, I am a defeated man."

Lady Clanwarren looked towards her husband and drew in her breath. And then, before she could open her lips, there was the sound of footsteps and Elvina came running through the French windows.

The sunshine was behind her, making her hair a halo of gold around her head.

Her small, slender graceful body was silhouetted against the light showing the new rounded maturity coming to her figure. Her eyes were shining and her lips parted with the speed at which she had come.

"Grandmama!" she cried. "Are these the roses you wanted me to pick?"

She came rushing towards them across the room, two perfect white blooms in her hand.

Then, only as she reached the hearthrug, only as she held the roses out to her grandmother, did she see that someone else stood there.

She raised her eyes and then, with a little gasp, she stood still, her head thrown back a little, her eyes looking up into Lord Wye's face.

No one said anything.

At Elvina's entrance Lord Wye had glanced at her quite casually and then the blood had drained away from his face.

Now he stood staring at her, it seemed to those watching, turned to stone. There was complete silence.

Two young people looked into each other's eyes and no one seemed capable of moving.

"*Elvina!*"

The words came hardly above a whisper from between Lord Wye's lips.

It was a tortured almost inarticulate sound and then suddenly he had put out his hands towards her, the roses had fallen to the floor and her fingers were in his.

"Elvina! Where did you come from? Where have you been? Why are you here?"

His questions tumbled over each other and yet she did not seem to hear them.

She was gazing at him with such a wonder and a glory in her face that her grandmother felt the tears start in her eyes.

"Why are you here?" Lord Wye managed to say again.

He was breathing deeply like a man who has swum against a tempestuous sea or climbed a steep mountainside.

"This is my granddaughter, Lord Wye," Lady Clanwarren said gently.

He did not take his eyes from Elvina's face.

"And your sister?" he questioned.

"Forgive me, it was a – lie," she answered, her voice very soft and sweet. "I have no sister – only a grandmother and grandfather. I should have told you the truth, but I was afraid lest they would not take me in."

"Why did you go away?"

"Because I could not stay as I was. I wanted to – to look different, to look like – myself."

"To look different?" he said wonderingly, as if the idea had never struck him. "But how?"

"Do you not see? Do you not see any difference?" she asked.

He looked down at her in a bemused fashion, his eyes glancing hastily at her ivory white neck and shoulders, at her little shell-like ears, her quivering mouth and then back again to her eyes.

"I don't see very much difference," he said.

Elvina gave a little laugh that was almost a sob.

"My – skin."

He looked at her again as if forcing himself to concentrate on what she was saying.

"It is whiter. Oh, you mean you are not Portuguese?"

"No, I am English."

"English!" he exclaimed. "And you live here? These are your grandparents? Then all my plans, all the things I have been thinking – "

"What were they?" she asked softly.

"I have been planning to send you to school."

"As Lady Cleone wished to do?"

"No, no, of course not," he said almost irritably. "Lady Cleone's ideas were ridiculous. *No!* To the best, the finest school in the land. To have you educated there while I waited for you."

"Waited – for – me?"

The question was like the sudden song of a lark rising into the sky. It was impossible for him to look anywhere save at her eyes.

They neither of them noticed that Lady Clanwarren had risen and, taking her husband's arm, had drawn him from the room.

They were alone, but they did not know it.

They could see nothing and nobody save each other.

"Why were you – waiting?" Elvina asked.

"Until you should grow up," he answered.

He felt her fingers quiver in his.

"But – why?"

She could hardly breathe the words and yet somehow they came from between her lips.

"I did not mean to tell you," he said, "but I have to. I have to make you understand. You must marry me! I love you, Elvina!"

She closed her eyes for a moment. The glory of it was too much to be borne. And then suddenly something snapped in him and he swept her into his arms.

"I love you! *I love you*!" he cried wildly. "All those days and nights when we were struggling to keep alive, that time together taught me that I cannot do without you. I want you! I need you! You belong to me!"

He looked down at her face and his voice deepened.

"I think I knew that we were meant for each other that moment when you looked across the table in the yacht and pleaded with me to let you stay. You are mine, Elvina! *Mine*! And I cannot let you go!"

She could feel his heart beating beneath her cheek and now she raised her head and looked up at him.

"Is it true?" she asked. "Really true that you are saying this to me? I am not dreaming?"

"You are awake, my little love. But we have to be sensible. I cannot marry a child."

"How long must we – wait?" she whispered.

"Do you suppose I have not been asking that question day after day while I have been looking for you?" he asked. "I suppose until you are seventeen. It will be hard, but we must do it."

"Seventeen!" she echoed, and then with a hint of laughter in her voice asked, "You are quite – sure that you do – want me?"

"Want you!" he answered. "Do you know what tortures you have put me through these last three weeks? I thought I should go mad when day after day went by and there was no sign of you. God knows what I imagined had happened! I used to walk my room at night thinking of you alone and unprotected in London. I used to try to send my thoughts towards you, believing that somehow, wherever you were, they would reach you."

"I think they – did," she said softly.

"And yet you did not come back to me."

"I had to wait, I had to make myself attractive – so that I could compete," she answered.

"Compete with whom?" he asked roughly. "There is no other woman in my life and never has been. You look to me as you have always looked, the most wonderful, the most adorable person I have ever known, the only woman I have ever loved."

He gave a sudden groan and held her tighter still.

"Oh, Elvina, grow up quickly!"

"I have," she answered him. "I have grown up. Do you not understand?"

He cupped his hand round her chin and raised her little face towards his.

"What are you saying to me?" he asked. "It's difficult to understand. I am just so happy that you are here."

"I am telling you that there is no need to – wait," she replied.

"Why? I may be very dense, but I don't understand."

She freed herself of his arms with a little twist of her body.

"Look at me," she insisted. "Look at me properly."

"You are lovely!" he exclaimed. "But you always were. Every night I would think of your little nose etched against the darkness, as it was that night in the tool shed. Do you remember?"

"Look at me," Elvina repeated.

"Why is your hair so gold?" he asked. "I thought it was dark, but somehow I cannot remember. I am so bemused. You always seemed like sunshine and light and laughter and happiness to me, Elvina."

She swayed at the passion and the longing in his voice.

Still she did not go to him.

"Look again," she persisted.

"You are not so thin. You have put on a little weight."

"Is that all?"

He looked at her again.

"Perhaps you look older. The new way you are doing your hair. It is that gown, or – " a sudden thought struck him. "Is that what you are trying to tell me? You are older? Was that another of your lies? Oh, Elvina, I always said that you were an imp of mischief!"

"Yes, it was another of my lies."

"Then how old are you?"

She heard the sudden tremble in his voice, the sudden yearning as a man who sees his goal ahead and yet is half-afraid it is a mirage.

"I am seventeen," she said softly.

He gave a shout of sheer unbridled triumph and then she was in his arms and he was kissing her wildly, not tenderly as a man kisses a child, but hungrily as a man kisses a woman whom he desires beyond all else in the world.

"I love you!" he cried. "Oh, Elvina, stop me. I shall frighten you. I shall drive you away again. But I want you so utterly. You are mine, as I told you. Mine alone! I don't have to wait. I can take you, make you my wife! Oh, my darling, say it is true, that this too is not a dream!"

She put up her arms and drew his head close down to hers.

"If it is a – dream," she whispered passionately, "let's go on – dreaming!"

OTHER BOOKS IN THIS SERIES

The Barbara Cartland Eternal Collection is the unique opportunity to collect all five hundred of the timeless beautiful romantic novels written by the world's most celebrated and enduring romantic author.

Named the Eternal Collection because Barbara's inspiring stories of pure love, just the same as love itself, the books will be published on the internet at the rate of four titles per month until all five hundred are available.

The Eternal Collection, classic pure romance available worldwide for all time.